# THE BOSELLI BRIDE

BY
SUSANNE JAMES

MILLS & BOON®

All the characters in this book have no existence outside the imagination of the author, and have no relation whatsoever to anyone bearing the same name or names. They are not even distantly inspired by any individual known or unknown to the author, and all the incidents are pure invention.

First published in Great Britain 2009
Paperback edition 2010
Harlequin Mills & Boon Limited,
Eton House, 18-24 Paradise Road, Richmond, Surrey TW9 1SR

© Susanne James 2009

ISBN: 978 0 263 87761 8

Set in Times Roman 10½ on 12¼ pt
01-0110-51896

Harlequin Mills & Boon policy is to use papers that are natural, renewable and recyclable products and made from wood grown in sustainable forests. The logging and manufacturing process conform to the legal environmental regulations of the country of origin.

Printed and bound in Spain
by Litografia Rosés, S.A., Barcelona

# THE BOSELLI BRIDE

# CHAPTER ONE

'WHY don't you go back to the hotel, Coral, and have a lie down…'? It *is* pretty stifling today.' Emily glanced sympathetically at her friend as they sauntered along the sun-hot streets of the capital.

'I think "pretty stifling" is a bit of an understatement—it must be all of forty degrees,' Coral said plaintively, taking off her hat for a second to wipe perspiration from her forehead. She sighed. 'Perhaps I will get a cab and go back… Do you have much more to do, Ellie?'

'Not really—but I'll look in on one more place before I call it a day,' Emily replied. She glanced at her watch. 'I'll be back before five o'clock, and then there'll be time for me to have a rest and a shower before we find somewhere for dinner.'

The two girls were staying at a small hotel in Rome on the outskirts of Trastevere. Emily was on one of her normal working assignments, where she had the task of vetting certain hotels and restaurants for the travel firm who employed her, and this was the first time she'd ever been accompanied abroad while on business. But Coral's long-term boyfriend, Steve, had recently dumped her and, in an attempt to cheer her friend up, Emily had suggested she come to

Rome, too. 'A complete change will do you good, Coral,' she'd said and, after a little persuasion, Coral had agreed.

Although her grasp of Italian was rather poor, Emily was determined to become sufficiently fluent to make herself well understood by the staff at all the places she'd been asked to investigate—while also expecting that their English could cope with the continuous influx of visitors from Britain.

Stopping for a moment to buy herself a cappuccino ice cream, she started to stroll up a side street which appeared almost completely shaded by the tall buildings on either side. She paused briefly to lick her tongue quickly around and around the smooth, creamy ice cream as it threatened to melt before she could eat it, then wandered on again somewhat listlessly. Perhaps she should have gone back to the hotel as well, she thought—but there was this one other restaurant she needed to visit before finishing for the day.

Soaking up the atmosphere of the ancient city, she wondered whether her parents had actually walked up this very street when they had done all their travelling. The thought of her mother, who had died so suddenly four years ago when she, Emily, was twenty-one, made the girl's eyes mist and she swallowed a painful lump in her throat. Even though her father, Hugh, had picked up the pieces of his life and carried on alone, she knew that he didn't find it easy… They'd been such a close couple, and wonderful parents to her and her brother, Paul. Paul was just a few years older than her, but he had a rather serious nature and outlook on life—which might be partly explained by his work as a lawyer. Emily wished that he was here now, so that she could give him a hug.

Lost in her own thoughts, her reverie was brought to a

sudden—and ignominious—halt as she almost fell over someone sitting on the pavement outside a small shop whose open-fronted entrance exhibited a colourful array of pottery and glass. Half-sitting, half-lying on a canvas chair with his long legs stretched out nonchalantly in front of him, his large-brimmed hat completely shading his face, he might have been fast asleep because he made no discernible movement as Emily paused to glance at the wares on offer. Slightly embarrassed at how close she'd come to nearly sitting on his lap, she cleared her throat and busied herself with picking up one or two items, even though she had no intention of buying anything. If she'd purchased something in every place she'd been sent to since working abroad, her small flat would be hopelessly overloaded. But then—there was always room for just one more jug, she thought.

Venturing just a little way inside the shop, she gingerly picked up a round, chunky marmalade jar—her father had started making his own marmalade, and she thought how he would love this.

'Unique.' The man's voice was cruelly seductive.

Turning quickly, Emily found herself looking way up into the blackest of black eyes—eyes which twinkled mischievously into her soft grey ones…. The inert figure outside had come to life! Standing now, he had removed his hat and his thick, dark and lustrous hair hung haphazardly over his forehead, while the deeply tanned skin of his outrageously handsome face shone slightly with perspiration.

'I'm sorry…?' Emily found herself fluttering inside like a silly schoolgirl! Come on, she thought, this isn't the first Italian male you've met! Get a grip!

'Unique,' he repeated, averting his gaze from hers just long enough to pick up one of the jars and to slowly turn it around in his long, sensuous fingers. 'Each one unique.'

Emily smiled inwardly. He was a man of few words, his somewhat sparse way of communicating clearly suggesting that his English was about as good as her Italian.

'They're…very…attractive,' she murmured, speaking slowly. 'How much…?'

Now he smiled down, his glistening, perfect teeth enlivening the density of his tan. Without taking his eyes from her, he pointed to the small price tag at the base of the jar, raising one eyebrow quizzically.

'Of course—I should have spotted that,' Emily said quickly, taking her purse from her bag.

'No problem.' He spoke carefully—and Emily thought, well, he'd obviously learned the necessary phrases to get by. So far he'd only uttered about six words, but he was doing all right. Quite well enough to run this small, unassuming shop. She smiled up at him, handing over her euros, conscious that his fingers seemed to linger on hers for several seconds longer than was necessary but admitting that she'd not objected to the feel of his hand on hers like that. He was not offensive in any way, just…just warm…warm and even affectionate. What she had seemed to need just then.

She watched as he carefully wrapped the jar in brown paper before putting it into a small bag. He handed it to her slowly.

'For you?' he asked.

Emily couldn't help smiling at him again. 'No. A gift,' she replied, her comments as economically spoken as his. 'For my father. He…he likes to make his own marmalade these days.' Now why had she bothered to tell the man that? He was only being polite. He didn't need to know her business.

'Ah, yes.' The dark eyes grew solemn for a moment. 'Your father… He is alone, yes?'

She hesitated. 'My mother died. Not so long ago,' she said quietly, and suddenly his brown hand caught hers again and squeezed it gently—not like before, but impulsively, sympathetically.

'I'm sorry,' he murmured, letting her go and moving away. Then his eyes twinkled again and the moment had gone.

Emily turned decisively. 'Thank you very much…for the jar,' she said.

He bowed his head slightly to one side. 'You are very welcome,' he replied formally.

Emily walked away and up the street, admitting that she felt strange inside. What on earth was the matter—had she got sunstroke? But that unlooked-for encounter with possibly the most overtly sensuous Italian male she'd ever spoken to had shaken her up. Had made her feel quite giddy. What on earth had they put in that ice cream?

With slightly narrowed eyes he watched her as she walked away. Of course he'd seen her coming up the street towards him a few minutes ago, his natural antennae homing in on her delectable appearance, on the cool, straight dress just above the knee, revealing gently tanned slim legs, her long fair hair falling casually onto her shoulders, her glitzy strappy sandals twinkling in the heat as she strolled. She was obviously in no hurry, he'd thought as he'd observed her enjoying her ice cream. She'd paused briefly a couple of times as she'd licked at the ice cream, then he'd watched as she'd nibbled at the last piece of the biscuit before taking a tissue from her bag to wipe her lips. He'd recognized at once that she was not of his own nationality—probably English, he'd thought, or German— or Swedish. A familiar shiver of desire had rippled right down his spine as he'd seen the slight figure come nearer, and he'd deliberately lowered his head even further on his chest while still maintaining his undisturbed scrutiny of her. And then she'd given him the perfect opportunity to come and stand close to her as she'd stopped to examine some of the merchandise on display. And to buy something. He had taken his time wrapping up what she had chosen, inhaling the light, tantalizing drift of her perfume.

Now, he sighed as he watched her disappear out of sight. She had been like a welcome apparition in the rather sickly afternoon heat, and now she had gone. He glanced at his watch, feeling somewhat irritable. He only had another hour here before someone came to relieve him, and then he could go and have a long, satisfying drink to cool himself down.

Emily had some difficulty finding the restaurant on her list that she wanted to visit—no one seemed to know where it was—but eventually she tracked it down and had a brief interview with the manager. It seemed a friendly, well patronized place, just the sort she herself might like to eat in, she thought and, taking away some menus and other literature, she hailed a taxi and went back to the hotel.

Coral was lying on her bed reading a magazine.

'Oh, good, you're back,' she said. 'Did you manage to finish what you had to do?' She stared at Emily for a second, thinking how pretty her friend looked. She had the same slim figure she'd had when she'd been in her teens. 'You look as cool as a cucumber, Ellie—and you're very lucky you don't burn in this sun,' she remarked. 'Not like me. With your fair skin you ought to look like a lobster.' She sighed. 'There's no justice.' Coral's red hair and freckled skin needed a lot of protection in these conditions.

'Well, I may not look burned up, but I feel it right

now—' Emily smiled '—so it's a cool shower for me.' She took a long cotton skirt and fresh top from the wardrobe and went into the bathroom. 'Shan't be long.'

Later, refreshed and looking forward to their evening, the two girls left the hotel and took a taxi to the centre of town.

'With your experience and expertise, you ought to know all the best places to eat,' Coral said as they strolled along the busy streets.

'I still have a lot to learn,' Emily said. 'I've only been sent here once before, but there'll certainly be plenty of choice.' They went on, passing one restaurant after another, the early evening atmosphere muted and relaxed, and presently they stopped for a moment outside a particularly well-lit place to examine the menu. 'This looks good,' she said. 'Shall we try it?'

They took their seats at a table outside under the sun awning and Coral sighed. 'Why does the thought of food always fill me with such delight?' she asked, glancing across at Emily. 'At this moment in time, I do not wish to be anywhere else, *with* anyone else,' she added meaningfully.

Emily smiled at the words, knowing that Coral had always loved food. But since the split with her boyfriend, Steve, a month ago, she had definitely started to look thinner—and it didn't suit her. Coral's normal appetite was legendary, and it went with her popularity and usually bright outlook on life.

'The only thing to complete this idyllic picture,' Coral said as she examined the menu, 'is for a drop-dead gorgeous Italian male to present himself at my feet and whisk me off to some exotic rendezvous. But not until I've had my meal,' she added.

Emily felt pleased that a change of scene seemed to be

having a positive effect on Coral's frame of mind. Her recent depression seemed to be less in evidence, anyway—at least for the moment. Coral and Steve had been an item for four years—with neither, apparently, wanting to commit themselves, when one day, out of the blue, he'd announced that enough was enough and he wanted to call it a day. To describe it as an emotional bombshell was an understatement and Emily had felt it too—the girls shared their lives in a flat together. It was horrible to see the normally happy-go-lucky Coral so downcast.

As she ran her finger along the huge menu, Emily frowned slightly. It was all very well thinking about other people's affairs and relationships…but what about her own love life? She had to admit that it didn't stand much scrutiny at the moment—and who could blame her for that? Her confidence in human relationships having a hope of surviving in the long-term had been shattered when Marcus, her last boyfriend, had been targeted by her best friend from university, who had made no secret of the fact that she'd always fancied Marcus. But it had never bothered Emily, who'd trusted him so naively…so, when he'd unbelievably succumbed to the determined charms of the other woman, Emily had suffered a bombshell all of her own. Then, it had been Coral's job to pick up the shattered pieces of her ego and her bruised heart. Emily sighed briefly as her thoughts ran on. The event was a whole year ago and, although she barely thought about him now, she'd been taught a hard lesson. Beware of those you thought you could trust. Especially handsome men, who were naturally attractive to the opposite sex.

Presently, they gave the young Italian waitress their order, and within a couple of minutes two large glasses of white wine arrived. Coral picked up hers straight away, beaming across at Emily.

'Cheers,' she said, taking a generous gulp, and Emily smiled back, picking up her own drink. It was good to have her friend's company on this trip, she thought. Even if she *was* beginning to get used to finding her own way around new places and fending for herself.

Coral leaned back in her chair and looked around. 'There seems so much talent everywhere,' she said, almost ruefully. 'I mean, just look at those two guys over there, Ellie— gorgeous or what?' She paused. 'Hey, they're looking at us… Do you think we might get lucky later on…?'

'Well, *you* might,' Emily said cheerfully, 'but count me out. I've got my busiest day tomorrow, and after we've eaten it'll be back to bed for me.'

'Spoilsport,' Coral said. 'Anyway, I was only joking.' But she continued staring across at the men, returning their rather suggestive smiles.

Emily said mildly, 'Don't encourage them, Coral. It'll really complicate matters if they think we're giving them the come-on.'

Soon their meal was put in front of them and for the next ten minutes Coral didn't say another word as she began rapidly consuming everything on her plate.

'This veal is so tender,' Emily said appreciatively, 'and I wish I knew what the dressing on the salad is. It's fantastic.'

'And I love, love, *love* these chips!' Coral said theatrically. 'I was so afraid we were only going to get pasta on this holiday.'

The portions were generous, so the girls decided that fruit and coffee would be all they'd need to complete the meal. But Coral insisted on ordering more wine, waving away Emily's protest.

'Don't be a party-pooper, Ellie,' she said beseechingly. 'We're on holiday, remember.'

'You are—I'm not,' Emily replied, but she drank the wine anyway. She certainly didn't want to be accused of being a drag. Anyway, Coral was having such a good time it was hard not to be affected by the girl's exuberance.

As they sat sipping their wine, the men whom Coral had been smiling at came over and, without asking, pulled out two chairs so that they could sit down.

'Is OK,' one of them said, 'to sit?' and, although Emily merely shrugged pleasantly, Coral was thrilled.

'Of course it's OK,' she said brightly, darting a quick glance at Emily.

Immediately, one of the men beckoned a waiter and insisted that the girls should have more wine. They were young—probably barely twenty years old, Emily thought—good-looking and well turned-out in their casual clothes, and it was obvious that they'd been encouraged by Coral's overtly friendly eye signals.

It didn't take long for the men to find out that the girls were English and on holiday and, in their halting attempts to make themselves understood, they became more and more animated, throwing their heads back and roaring with laughter at the mistakes they were making. But when one of them leaned across and took hold of Emily's hand, looking into her eyes and telling her how beautiful she was, the girl had had enough. While she was quite ready to go along with this—up to a point, for Coral's sake—it was becoming clear that this was going to lead to a situation she definitely did not want. She took her hand away, glancing at her watch.

'Well—great to have met you,' she said, 'but we have to go now.'

'Oh—no—no,' her admirer said. 'Is too early…'

Emily looked helplessly at Coral, hoping for some

support, but her friend refused to meet her gaze, clearly enjoying the situation, and for a few moments Emily felt at a loss. The men were only being friendly and she had no sense of being threatened. Yet this was the very thing she had wanted to avoid. How was she going to get out of it without appearing to snub these local lads?

And then her good fairy alighted on her shoulder, literally, as the warm hand of the handsome Italian she'd met earlier in the day rested on her bare arm for a second. He looked down into her rather startled gaze and smiled the smile that set her heart racing.

'We meet again,' he said calmly. 'I was sitting inside in the bar having a drink and saw you come in.' He paused. 'Is—is everything all right?' The words were uttered in perfect English, which had the effect of throwing Emily off balance for a moment. What she'd thought of earlier as his halting ability with the language was obviously a ploy he used in order to avoid having to make tiresome conversation with customers! But she admitted to feeling relieved that he'd turned up then—because now the situation was different—and the younger men saw it at once, standing up almost deferentially.

''*Giorno,* Giovanni,' the men said, almost in unison. He was obviously well known, Emily thought—and why not? He ran a local shop, and these were local youths. She smiled up at him.

'Oh, hello again,' she said. 'We…were just explaining to these…guys…that we are actually just leaving now…'

'*Giovanni*' spoke in rapid Italian to the men, who answered back in the same way, all three laughing loudly and clearly enjoying a joke—probably at her and Coral's expense, Emily thought—and then they were gone, smiling back as they went, leaving Giovanni standing there alone. He looked down at the girls, treating Coral to one of his disarming grins before introducing himself, holding out his hand to each of them in turn.

'My name is Giovanni,' he said, 'but my friends call me Joe…Gio.' He paused, his eyes flickering over Emily's upturned face.

Quickly, she said, 'Oh—I'm Emily, and this is Coral. We're only here for a few days—on a sort of holiday…' she went on rather stumblingly, aware that her friend was staring at her open-mouthed. Not just because it was obvious that Giovanni was somehow known to Emily, but also because he was looking so stunningly handsome she knew that the girl's curiosity would be killing her. Emily knew she had some explaining to do!

'Um…do sit down…Giovanni…' she said hesitantly, and immediately he pulled out a chair. She looked across at Coral. 'I bought a lovely present for my father at Giovanni's shop this afternoon,' she began, 'and that's when I met…Giovanni…Gio…'

Although Coral might have been disappointed at the hasty exit the younger men had just made, she was so entranced at the most recent arrival she could hardly speak! He was wearing well-cut jeans and a loose, immaculate white cotton shirt open at the neck, exhibiting a teasing expanse of muscular brown chest. His hair was stylishly untidy, one or two dark fronds falling over his broad forehead. And his bewitching eyes were fringed by long, curling lashes. But when he leaned across and took Coral's hand in his briefly, saying, 'I am so delighted to meet you, Coral,' Emily thought her friend was going to faint!

'Oh…' Coral said at last. 'Pleased to meet you, Gio.' She darted a quick glance at Emily, as if to say—*Well, you might have said something*—before giving the man her close attention. And his perfect English, with only the occasional mouth-watering Italian accent, made conversation easy—and wonderfully entertaining, as he turned on the full power of his Latin charm. He beckoned to the drinks waiter and turned to Emily.

'May we celebrate our acquaintance?' he asked. 'What would you like to drink—and you, Coral…? What may I order for you?'

'I'd like another coffee, please,' Emily said firmly. She'd already had several generous glasses of wine. Any more would be too many, she thought. But Coral had no such problem, and soon she was sipping at yet another large glass of the expensive bubbles as she regaled Giovanni with her life story, allowing Emily to add one or two comments about herself while he listened intently.

Presently, Emily decided that for her the evening was over. 'I want to go back to the hotel now, Coral,' she said. 'It's late.'

'Where are you staying?' Giovanni asked casually, and when they told him he said, 'I can take you, if you like. My car is just a few minutes away.'

'Oh, lovely!' Coral said at once, but Emily interrupted firmly.

'Thank you, but we can easily get a taxi. We wouldn't want to bother you.' She stood up and shot a warning glance at Coral, who stood up as well. Then she held out her hand. 'It's been very…pleasant…to meet you…Gio,' she said. 'And thanks for the coffee.'

He smiled at her, tilting his head briefly to one side. 'You're welcome,' he said. He hesitated. 'By the way, if you have trouble locating the places you need to visit tomorrow, I'll be at the shop, so you know where to find me. I can always point you in the right direction.'

'Oh…thank you, but I'm sure I'll manage,' Emily said.

'Why didn't you accept his offer of a lift?' Coral demanded as they were driven swiftly back to the hotel in a taxi.

'Because we don't know him, Coral!'

'He wasn't exactly a stranger…'

'As good as,' Emily replied.

But later, as Emily listened to Coral's gentle snoring from the other bed, she instinctively felt that there would have been no need to fear Giovanni's intentions. He was clearly a well known member of the local community and, if the younger men's reaction was anything to go by, highly respected.

Emily turned over, flinging her arm across her pillow. Behind her closed lids she could still see those ruinously seductive eyes gazing at her. Then she half sat up, pushing her hair away from her face. This would not do, she thought. She was here chiefly on business, not to indulge herself in sensitive thoughts about the first Italian who'd paid her any special attention. It was just a shame that she and Giovanni would probably never meet again…especially as there were only two days to go before they returned to England.

Back in his luxury flat in the heart of the city, Giovanni dragged his shirt over his head and unbuckled his jeans before going into the bathroom to shower. What a piece of good luck that he'd come across Emily again. She might have gone to any one of the countless restaurants on offer, or indeed might have already been on her way back home. And what luck that fate had given him the opportunity to approach her without causing any offence. He'd observed the young men attach themselves to the two girls, and had spotted at once that Emily had seemed uncomfortable about it. She'd certainly not appreciated the rather clumsy gesture she'd received from one of them. It was that which had made Giovanni intervene.

He stared at himself in the mirror for a second, a slight grin on his rugged face. He met many lovely women all the time, and this was hardly the first occasion that his masculine propensities had been briefly shaken and stirred. But, somehow, this felt different… He suddenly felt alive inside again, the persistent sense of guilt which he'd been suffering for the last eighteen months lessening slightly. He bit his lip. He was being introspective again, he thought. He must stop it. Wasn't it time to give himself an emotional break and start looking forward, instead of back? And he was not going to deny that Emily had lit a particular spark in him which was both exciting and unexpected. On so short an acquaintance he was, quite simply, enchanted by her. She was not only beautiful, she was…thoughtful…wistful, maybe…some other quality that he couldn't quite identify, but everything about her made him want to hold her and protect her. He had never, ever felt that instant, deep attraction to a woman before in his life—and the realization came as something of a shock.

Stepping into the shower, he let the water rush in cool, satisfying waves over the length of his taut, muscular body before beginning to soap himself vigorously. At least he knew where she'd be staying for the next few days, but he didn't have long and he wanted to know more about this Englishwoman before it was too late.

He finished showering, then knotted the huge white towel around his waist and padded barefoot into his bedroom, feeling elated. Feeling eighteen again. Emily Sinclair had definitely sprinkled some magic dust over him that day, he admitted—and who knew what may lie ahead? Didn't all his friends call him 'Lucky Gio'?

# CHAPTER TWO

'OH, WHAT a night I've had!'

Coral sat on the edge of her bed with her head in her hands, then peered through her fingers at Emily, who was barely awake. 'But I'm glad that I don't appear to have disturbed *you*,' she added a trifle sarcastically.

Emily sat up and stared at her friend sleepily. 'No, I didn't hear a thing. In fact, I had the best sleep I've had in ages. But—what happened—or shouldn't I ask?'

'Oh, it's just that I've been in and out of the bathroom for the entire night,' Coral replied. 'I suppose it was something I ate for supper,' she added.

'Well, we had the same thing and it didn't affect me,' Emily said mildly, thinking that it was probably more to do with the amount Coral had had to drink. She'd almost single-handedly consumed the bottle of expensive wine which Giovanni had bought, and she'd had a lot before that. 'Do you think you can manage breakfast?' she asked doubtfully. The girl was still looking very white-faced.

'Don't! Don't mention food!' Coral said theatrically. 'It'll be nil by mouth for me today.' She got up slowly and went across to the window, clasping her stomach. 'It looks as if it's going to be another scorcher,' she said, 'but I shan't be coming with you, Ellie. I couldn't trust myself to be anywhere but here for the next few hours.' She turned to glance at Emily. 'Do you mind?'

'Of course I don't mind,' Emily said at once. 'But you're probably over the worst.' She climbed out of bed, yawning. 'I'll ring your mobile at lunchtime to see if you're able to come and meet me later.'

As soon as she'd had her breakfast, Emily took a few moments to read the instructions she'd been given. There were two hotels and two restaurants on her list for today and, although her map-reading skills weren't particularly impressive, she felt reasonably confident that she'd be able to get around. A couple of the places looked fairly close to each other, but the others seemed more spread out.

After feeling as if she'd walked fifty miles on the unyielding pavements, Emily had tracked down the two more central establishments before deciding to stop at a small café for a few minutes to make some notes. And to order a long glass of freshly squeezed orange juice.

Sitting with her pad on her knee, she sipped her drink, staring pensively out at the fast-moving traffic. She was doing OK, she thought, feeling quite pleased with herself—even if she *had* gone round in circles when given conflicting directions by two passers-by. But she decided that she'd hail a taxi to take her to the next stop—a rather nice-looking hotel, if the description on her notes was anything to go by.

Standing uncertainly on the pavement, she held out her hand as one cab after another swept past her, obviously all occupied, and after several fruitless minutes she began to walk a little way up the street before trying her luck again. She saw another one approaching her rapidly and, stepping off the kerb in order to get the driver to stop, she stumbled and almost fell as he, too, roared past her. Emily bit her lip in frustration—why was it proving so difficult? she asked herself, beginning to feel hot and bothered all over again.

Suddenly, a sleek black car pulled up alongside her and, glancing in quickly at the driver, she felt a rush of pleasure—and relief—when she saw who it was.

'*Buon giorno, signorina,*' Giovanni said through the open window, a roguish smile on his lips, his black eyes unashamedly taking in her appearance.

'Oh…hello, Giovanni—I mean, Joe…' Emily replied, hardly believing her luck. He'd be sure to offer to help find the place she was looking for—and in this heat she wouldn't be turning him down.

Without switching off the engine, he got out of the car and came around to open the passenger door for her. Well, well, well—Lady Luck was on his side again, he thought. It was as if she had been planted neatly on that pavement for him to offer her a ride. He didn't usually drive his car around the city at this time of day.

He got in beside her, turning to look at her for a second, noting her flushed cheeks and aware that she seemed out of breath. 'You were obviously trying to get a taxi,' he said. Well, there couldn't have been any other reason for her to stand there alone with her arms in the air. 'It can be difficult sometimes,' he added.

'So I see,' Emily replied as they drew away smoothly. 'None of them seem to need my custom today.' She leaned her head back and sighed, grateful for the air-conditioning—and to be with someone who knew where he was going. 'I need to visit two hotels today… My work involves assessing places that might meet all the criteria for British visitors,' she explained, 'and I don't know how to get to either of these.'

'Well, what a good thing I'm not at the shop this afternoon,' Giovanni said, 'so I can take you wherever you want to go.' Effortlessly, he pulled the car to the side of the road for a moment and looked across at her. 'What names are you looking for?'

Emily handed him the sheet of paper with the instructions and a small map, and after a few seconds he nodded. 'They're a bit out of the way,' he conceded, 'but easy enough to find. That's if you…are happy…for me to take you,' he added.

Emily looked at him quickly, realizing that today it hadn't struck her that the man was still the stranger that he'd been last night when she'd refused his offer of a lift. So why did she feel so relaxed…so happy…to be sitting alongside him now? She turned to look in front of her. 'If you're sure it's not inconveniencing you, Gio, I'd be very grateful,' she said simply.

'Which travel company are you with?' Giovanni wanted to know as they drove away and, when Emily told him, he nodded. 'They're well known,' he said briefly. 'How long have you worked for them?'

'Almost a year,' Emily replied.

'And before that?'

'Oh, I had a couple of years with a small art gallery in London,' she said, glancing across at the handsome profile, the strong neck and firm chin. His white shirt exposed heart-throbbing muscular arms and shoulders which tensed and rippled as he moved. She swallowed, looking away. 'And what about you?' she asked, thinking that it was his turn to answer some questions. 'How long have you owned the shop?'

He grinned without looking at her. 'Oh, it's not mine,' he said. 'It belongs to a friend. I just mind the place for him from time to time.'

There was silence for a few moments after that and Emily thought—well, that didn't say much. If it wasn't his shop, what else did he do?

'So, when you're not selling beautiful marmalade jars…?' she enquired.

'My friend also owns the restaurant you were dining in last night,' he said, 'and I help out there, too, in the bar sometimes—but mostly I manage his paperwork for him.' He paused. 'By the way,' he went on, changing the subject, 'where is—Coral—today?'

'Oh, I'm afraid Coral might have had too much sun yesterday,' Emily said. She wasn't going to go into details. 'So she decided to stay at the hotel and rest for a few hours…which reminds me—I must ring her to see if she's feeling any better.'

Taking her mobile from her bag, Emily dialled Coral's number and was relieved that her friend answered almost immediately and sounded her old self.

'Good,' Emily said into the mouthpiece, 'I'll be back about six o'clock and we'll go out to supper later—if you're still feeling OK… What? Oh—I'm phoning from… from… I'm in a car on my way to one of those hotels, but once I'm there it shouldn't take long,' she added as she rang off.

Now why hadn't she told Coral that it was Giovanni's car that she was sitting in? she asked herself as she replaced her phone in her bag. And Giovanni must have been thinking the same thing because he gave her a wicked sidelong glance and said bluntly, 'Is my name a dirty word then, Emily? You're not…ashamed…of me, I hope?'

Emily felt her cheeks beginning to burn. 'Of course not!' she said. 'It…it was somehow difficult to try and explain to Coral how you…I mean…how…I'll tell her later, of course.' The fact was that Coral had fallen madly in love with Giovanni and when they'd got back last night hadn't stopped going on and on about him until the small hours. If Emily had said, *Guess what? Giovanni just happened to be passing by and now I'm sitting in his fantastic car and yes, he's just as gorgeous as he was last night!* Coral would have demanded to know how *that* had happened, and her shriek of amazed jealousy would have been deafening and very difficult to explain to the man in the driving seat!

It took about twenty minutes to reach the quite imposing hotel, and Giovanni glanced across at Emily. 'Do you have an appointment, or do you just turn up unannounced?' he asked.

'It varies,' Emily replied. 'It's quite good not to let them know when you're coming, for obvious reasons, but I usually do ring first. Let's hope the manager is available today. I'm hoping to see Signor Saracco, but in any case I can get a good feel of the place and see if it's the sort which our clients might approve of.'

They got out of the car and together they went into the large foyer. This would obviously have to feature in the brochure for one of their more expensive holidays, Emily thought, looking around her at the impressive glass cabinets containing luxurious clothing and jewellery. The girl standing behind the huge oak reception desk looked up as they entered, her eyes glancing briefly at Emily, but lingering for a lot longer on Giovanni, immediately captivated by his ruthlessly seductive appeal.

Emily stepped forward. *'Parla inglese?'* she asked, and the woman nodded hesitantly.

'A leetle,' she replied.

In the following few moments it was obvious that the

receptionist was having a struggle with the language, and Emily made a mental note of the fact. It would be important for British visitors to feel comfortable at this early point, she thought, and for any queries they might have to be dealt with efficiently. Then Giovanni spoke quietly to the girl and for what seemed like ten minutes to Emily they conversed rapidly in Italian, the receptionist clearly relieved to be speaking her own language, laughing excitedly now and then—and also obviously enjoying talking to the handsome visitor. Then he glanced down at Emily.

'This young lady is only standing in for the permanent receptionist,' he explained, 'owing to illness. She only started today and says it's been the longest morning of her life. Another girl is coming in tomorrow, apparently. She is only seventeen,' he added, and Emily was amazed. 'Carla'—for that was the name on the identity tag the girl was wearing—looked at least in her mid-twenties. She was immaculately dressed, her black outfit pristine and enlivened with gold jewellery, her dark hair swept back elegantly. 'I also asked if Signor Saracco was available, and she says that he is due back in one hour,' Giovanni went on. 'Do you want to hang on that long, or shall we find the other place first?' He paused. 'I don't know about you, but I didn't have any lunch. They do very good light meals, served all afternoon, so Carla tells me…'

Suddenly, the thought of sitting down to a gentle Italian repast sounded just what she needed and Emily smiled, realizing that her 'lunch' had been that glass of orange juice. 'I'd love something to eat,' she said, 'and we might as well wait for the manager now that we're here.'

'Good,' he said at once, cupping her elbow in his hand and leading her towards the other end of the entrance hall where late lunches were being served.

Without looking back, Emily knew that Carla would be watching them. The young girl had been instantly flattered by Giovanni's kindly attention to her, flashing her artificially long eyelashes at him as he'd looked across at her. And Emily could quite see how any female would be touched by his attitude. He'd been attentive, understanding…and deliciously sensuous, yet not creepy or overpowering. She'd give him full marks for the way in which he demonstrated his particular art—or was it craft?

He led her to a small round table in the corner, by a window which looked out across a beautifully green lawn. In a lazy circular movement, a hose was lightly playing water over the grass and Emily glanced up at Giovanni as he held out a chair for her to sit down.

'They must employ a lot of staff to keep this place up to standard,' she said. 'It does seem a very well run establishment.'

For a few moments they studied a copy of the menu, then both decided on something called the House Special, which was ravioli accompanied by freshly cooked spinach.

'I hope the service is good,' Giovanni remarked as he clicked his fingers to attract the attention of the drinks waiter, 'because I'm starving.'

Emily had to admit that she was beginning to feel the same way, and soon they were tucking into what turned out to be a really delicious version of the simple Italian dish. 'When I do ravioli at home,' she said, running her knife around her plate to scoop up the last of the sauce, 'it doesn't taste nearly as good as this.'

Giovanni smiled across at her, realizing how much he was enjoying the company of this Englishwoman whom he barely knew. His eyes narrowed briefly as he continued watching her. Although she was not cold towards him, he thought—no, not at all—he sensed a sort of protective film around her persona which seemed to exclude him. So why didn't he stick with his own kind? he asked himself. It wouldn't take long for that young receptionist to respond to his male ego!

Emily looked up at him now and he smiled, thinking that there was a little time to go before the manager turned up. Time to find things out.

'So,' he said smoothly, finishing the last of his beer, 'are there any more like you at home, Emily? Or are you an only child?'

'I have a brother,' Emily replied, folding her napkin and sitting back contentedly. 'He's a lawyer, and slightly older than me.' She paused. 'Although we both live and work in London, we don't see as much of each other as we'd like—there never seems enough time, somehow.'

'One must always make time for relationships,' Giovanni said, his expression darkening momentarily.

'Are your parents alive?' Emily wanted to know.

'I still have my mother with me,' he replied, 'but my father died ten years ago.'

So, Emily thought, they were both semi-orphans. 'Does your mother live in Rome with you?' she asked.

'No, we have a family home in the country, a few miles outside,' he said. 'She is happy there—though she sometimes comes into the city and stays at my flat when she feels like it.' He paused. 'And your father? You told me that he is alone now, but where does he live?'

'In the same house in Hampshire where my parents lived all their married life,' Emily replied, wishing that she hadn't had that small glass of white wine.

There was silence for a few moments, then he said

casually, 'And what about your love life, Emily—you have a partner longing for your return?'

Emily was a bit taken aback at the way he'd put the question—she didn't usually discuss her 'love life' with anyone! 'No, I do not have a partner—at the moment,' she said coolly, and he looked at her quizzically. There was a fleeting expression on her face which he couldn't interpret, didn't understand... Surely there must be a long queue of men lusting for her? he thought.

And Emily, looking out of the window thoughtfully, would not be telling him about Marcus—that was all in the past. And she was surviving life without specific male company too, she thought. Life was blissfully uncompli- cated now. Life was OK, wasn't it? She swallowed. It was time to talk of other things.

Just then a murmuring of voices coming from the re- ception area made them both glance up as three men, dressed formally, entered. Immediately, Giovanni stood up—he'd obviously seen someone he knew, Emily thought, and almost at once the taller one of the trio came over to them. He was about forty-five or so, Emily guessed, and extremely good-looking.

'Giovanni,' he began, his hand outstretched in greeting, and there followed a rapid exchange of Italian between the two of them. Then Giovanni looked down at Emily.

'Um...allow me to introduce you, Emily,' he said. 'This is...Aldo.' And to the man he added, 'The young lady is Emily. She is here on business.'

Aldo took Emily's hand in his and looked down at her, his searching Italian eyes seeming to unwrap every bit of her at a single glance. 'I am charmed to meet you, Emily,' he said smoothly, not letting her go, but turning his head to Giovanni. 'Another delightful creature to add to your list, my friend?' he said, and the remark seemed almost sinister to Emily. It held a definite touch of spite. She looked uncertainly at Giovanni—whose expression was non-committal, but there was suddenly a very cool atmosphere—and it seemed obvious that there was no love lost between these two.

After some more rather stilted discussion between them, Aldo made his gracious departure and joined his friends at a table at the opposite end of the room. Giovanni looked across at Emily as he sat down again.

'Well, I did not expect that,' he said, 'and I must apologize that we did not speak in English.'

Emily shrugged. 'Doesn't matter,' she said. 'Is he—is Aldo—a friend? You've known him a long time?'

Giovanni grimaced briefly. 'Too long,' he said.

'You don't like him?' she asked.

He shrugged. 'I neither like nor dislike him,' he replied casually. He paused. 'The more important point is that he resents me… He does not like me.'

No, Emily thought—she'd seen that straight away. 'Well, sometimes certain…friends…just don't fit somehow, do they?' she said. 'It's impossible to get on with each and every one of them.'

Giovanni nodded. 'Oh, I do OK with friends,' he said. 'They're no problem. Families are different.' He glanced over at the three men, who were giving the waiter their order for drinks. 'Aldo is family, unfortunately,' he said, a note of resignation in his voice. 'He's my uncle. My father's younger brother.'

'Oh,' Emily said, wondering why Giovanni hadn't mentioned that when they'd been introduced. Then she shrugged inwardly. She knew that Italians were known to be great family people, but even in the best of families there'd be bound to be friction now and then. She glanced at her watch. It must surely be time for the manager to return, she thought.

'You speak wonderful English, Gio,' she said, changing the subject. 'You've obviously spent a lot of time in the UK.'

'Explained by the fact that I was educated mostly there,' he said briefly.

Now, why did it surprise her, Emily asked herself, that he'd gone to school in England? 'Where did you go?' she asked him.

'Boarding school in Surrey, then Marlborough College in Wiltshire, followed by London University. And, before you ask, I gained a Masters in Business Law.'

Emily was almost bowled over by all this information! Despite being born in Italy, and in appearance and attitude being a perfect example of typical Latin charm, he was nearly as English as she was herself! She almost laughed out loud at the thought.

'So,' she said, 'if you only help out at the shop, and at your friend's bar when you're in Rome, where else do you work?' she asked. 'Where has all that education led you?'

He waited a moment before reaching into his pocket and handing her a small business card. 'Oh, I help my mother with a…um…family concern in Rome,' he said. 'Which means I have to come to the UK every now and again,' he added briefly.

Emily looked down at the card he'd handed her. *Giovanni Boselli,* she read. *Financial Consultant,* followed by his qualifications and the telephone number and address of the London office he apparently used. An address which was just a few streets away from her own office in Mayfair!

# CHAPTER THREE

'WELL, I think that's everything sorted—thanks to you, Gio,' Emily said, glancing across at him as they travelled back into the city later. 'It would have taken me a lot longer to find my own way around.'

'My pleasure,' he said easily. 'And—you were satisfied with both hotels?'

'Perfectly,' she replied. 'I shall be able to put ticks in all the right boxes.' She leaned her head back, feeling satisfied with the day's work. 'It was lucky for me that you happened to be free this afternoon—and also that you saw me trying to hail a taxi,' she added.

He looked across at her and grinned. 'Lucky for me, too,' he said. 'I've certainly enjoyed seeing you in action, Emily. You knew exactly how to handle those two managers, leaving them in no doubt what you expected— what your clients expected—of holiday accommodation.'

Emily was genuinely pleased at what he'd just said. Although she'd never been particularly shy or retiring, she'd had to get used to meeting complete strangers in foreign places, and assess their establishments without causing offence. And it could be difficult sometimes, when she could see straight away that some were totally unsuitable and would not get her recommendation.

It was six-thirty before Giovanni drew up outside the hotel and, switching off the engine, he said casually, his eyes glinting mischievously, 'As a small reward for having given you my undivided attention this afternoon, may I have the pleasure of taking you and Coral out for supper later?' he asked.

'Oh, but…I've already taken up far too much of your time, Giovanni,' Emily began, and he interrupted.

'Which I have very much enjoyed—as I've already said. So—why not make a day of it?' He paused. 'You're going home tomorrow, aren't you?'

'Yes,' Emily said, realizing that, for the very first time since she'd been doing all this travelling, she felt regretful that the trip wasn't going to be extended for a few more days. And she was honest enough to admit that meeting Giovanni had something to do with that!

'Well, I must speak to Coral about it,' she said. 'But thank you for the offer,' she added, knowing full well that her friend would be ecstatic at the thought of spending the evening with Giovanni.

He tilted his head to one side in acknowledgement of her words. 'You've got my card,' he reminded her, 'and my mobile number is on that. Give me a ring after you've mulled things over, and if you decide to accept my invitation I could pick you up at, say, eight-thirty or nine and take you to a place you'd probably never come across on your own—but which I can guarantee you'd like. But—' he touched her arm briefly '—don't worry if you decide to have an early night instead.' He paused. 'There'll be other occasions.' His lips parted in a brief knowing smile.

As soon as Emily got back to the room, she was almost

bowled over by Coral's excited welcome. 'Oh—hi, Ellie!' the girl exclaimed. 'Had a good day?' And, without waiting for a reply, she went on, 'You'll never guess what—I've pulled! We're going out tonight!'

Emily sat down on the edge of the bed for a second and looked up at Coral—who had obviously fully recovered, her eyes shining with girlish excitement. 'Go on—en-lighten me. What have you been up to?' she asked, a faint note of resignation in her voice.

'Honestly, I haven't been up to anything!' Coral ex-claimed. 'But this afternoon I was feeling so much better that I went down to Reception to order a tray of tea and that *gorgeous* guy—Nico—was on duty. You know, the one we've spoken to a couple of times?'

'Yes, of course I know who you mean,' Emily said. Yet another dashing and attentive Italian, she thought.

'Well, we sort of got chatting,' Coral went on, 'and I said I didn't know Rome very well and guess what—he wants to take us out to show us the sights. He's off duty at eight o'clock! What do you think of that?' She looked at Emily searchingly. 'It might be fun, Emily—and it *is* our last night.'

Emily got up and went over to put her laptop in the wardrobe, then turned to Coral. 'Strangely enough, I've had an invitation for us as well,' she said lightly, before going on to explain how Giovanni had arrived and had escorted her to the hotels on her list. 'And he's asked if we'd like to have dinner with him tonight,' she added.

Coral was speechless—but only for a second. 'How weird—that he should have turned up at just the right moment,' she said. 'But—now we've got *two* invites! Choices, choices!' She paused, thinking it over for a moment. 'But—it'll work perfectly, Ellie. I mean, I wouldn't want to turn Nico down—not after he was so sweet to me this afternoon—and you can't possibly disappoint Giovanni. That wouldn't be fair, since he's obviously been so wonderful to you today. So there you are—we'll go our separate ways tonight…and compare notes later!' she added darkly.

Emily smiled, shaking her head briefly at Coral's excitement. Her friend was obviously going to make the most of this final bit of her holiday—and what better way to end it than to be escorted around town by the handsome Nico?

Presently, as she washed away the day's dust under a cool shower, Emily couldn't help feeling pleased for Coral. Having an unexpected date was just the sort of thing to add a little sparkle to a holiday, she thought, and her friend was quite old enough—and sensible enough—to treat it as the light-hearted, inconsequential thing it was. And Emily had to admit that the thought of spending her last evening with Giovanni—just the two of them—held a little sparkle of its own! And why not? The occasional fleeting evening spent with an attractive man was the sort of thing which pleased her these days… No expectations, nothing heavy, which might threaten to cloud the long-term plan for her life. Go with the flow, but keep things cool—that was the best way.

Later, dressed in her white slim-leg cotton trousers and ocean-green low-necked top, Emily tripped lightly down the steps of the hotel to find Giovanni standing at the bottom waiting for her. Looking up, he grinned slowly, taking in every detail of her appearance and making no secret of his admiration.

'You are a very beautiful woman, Emily,' he murmured, and although Emily knew very well that easy compliments flew from the lips of amorous Italians like flocks of migrating birds, coming from Giovanni it seemed different. It seemed genuine, and she accepted it graciously.

'Thank you…Giovanni…' she said, lingering over his name for a second. He was so obviously a 'Giovanni' rather than a 'Joe', she thought briefly. That rather blunt derivative of his name could only be thanks to one of his English friends and somehow, to her, it didn't suit him. And tonight she could have added that he, too, was worth more than one glance. His black, well-fitting designer trousers were teamed with an ivory cotton shirt, casually open, showing off his golden chest. He obviously liked dressing well, Emily thought.

She glanced across at him as he drove them into town. 'Coral asked me to thank you again, for including her in tonight,' she said. 'As I explained on the phone, she'd already accepted an invitation which she didn't feel able to change.'

He looked back at her, his dark eyes glinting in the reflection from the brightly lit dials of the dashboard. 'No worries,' he said easily, thinking that, with another woman, he might have said that he was very happy to have her all to himself, so that he could treat her to the undivided attention that was his norm with alluring females. But he decided not to say that, happy to relax in the comfortable silence that seemed to exist between them. He frowned briefly. He had known so many women in his life—had always regarded the female sex as treasures to be valued. But would he ever meet a woman who didn't have an ulterior motive in wanting to belong to his family? That was what haunted him.

Feeling annoyed at his thoughts, he leaned forward to adjust something in front of him. The evening ahead was one to enjoy, for heaven's sake! And he was determined to do just that—and to make sure that Emily had a good time, too. When he'd first seen her yesterday—was it only yesterday? he asked himself—she'd had the usual instant effect on him, arousing an animal instinct of wanting to get close, even to possess. But there was this elusiveness about her which continued to intrigue him. And he had to penetrate it somehow, if only to convince himself that he could find out what it was, what lay behind the rather enigmatic expression he'd noted on her fine, perfect features.

Realizing that they'd not exchanged a word for the last few minutes, Emily said, without looking across at him, 'I hope today hasn't been too boring for you, Giovanni. I'm sure there were far more interesting things for you to do than transporting me around and hanging about...'

He interrupted her at once. 'I'm seldom bored, Emily. And I certainly wasn't today. I'm only too pleased that I was able to be of some use to you.'

'That's what you seem to do quite a lot of—being of use to people,' Emily said. 'Your friend who owns the shop and the restaurant seems to make good use of you when you're in Rome.' Now she did look across at him, chiding herself for the sensuous pleasure she was experiencing at being close to him, of seeing the strong brown hands on the steering wheel, his taut, muscular thighs visible beneath the fine fabric of his trousers. She swallowed, trying to think of Coral, and where Nico might be taking *her* tonight.

'Oh, well, my friends are good to me too, when I need them,' he said. Then, 'Are you hungry, Emily—would you like dinner straight away, or shall we go for a walk first?'

'I'd like to eat now—then maybe walk off my meal later!' Emily replied. 'Lunch does seem quite a long time ago.'

'Good. That suits me, too.' He smiled at her with that certain, gentle smile which had the effect of making Emily's pulse quicken. It *was* true, she thought—that Italian men had that certain something which could melt a woman's heart. She'd never really believed it, but now she was experiencing it first-hand... Giovanni exuded that courteous roguishness which personified the Italian male.

After he'd parked the car, they strolled along side by side, through streets which—although less busy—still seemed to ooze with the warm friendliness of the timeless city. They passed one or two families with small children in tow, couples sightseeing hand in hand, and now and then a cheerful group of young Italian men, maybe hopeful of a romantic assignation later, all adding to the laid-back atmosphere of the evening.

Walking along beside Giovanni, Emily felt a surge of unexpected happiness ripple through her. Being in the sole company of the most handsome man she'd ever laid eyes on was something she had not anticipated when she and Coral had left Heathrow the other day. She was not meant to be here enjoying herself—she was employed purely on a business basis. And she realized that it was the first time since starting the job that anyone had invited her out, or treated her as Giovanni was doing. She met plenty of pleasant—and not so pleasant—people during the course of an assignment, but no one had ever asked her out to dinner or treated her other than formally. But maybe that was down to her, she acknowledged. Although there were certain guidelines laid down by the company which she should conform to—mostly in her own interests—she was also aware that she seemed to have developed a natural antipathy to showing undue familiarity with people—notably with men. She hoped she wasn't thought of as stand-offish. Then she shrugged inwardly. So what? It was far safer, emotionally and in every other way, to keep slightly detached, to keep her distance. To try and enjoy life on the margins.

But, despite these thoughts, Emily was acutely aware that, although he was walking very closely by her side, Giovanni had not attempted to take her hand in his—and for a ridiculous moment she wished that he would! She could still recall the touch of his fingers on hers as he'd passed over the gift she'd bought at the shop yesterday— strong, protective fingers, sensitive and warm. Then she bit her lip. These thoughts must be thanks to the relaxed evening atmosphere, or to the occasional sight of two young lovers, their bodies entwined, as they passed, she thought.

He glanced down at her. 'Although I don't know your particular likes and dislikes, Emily,' he said, 'I'm pretty sure you'll approve of my choice of venue for tonight. There are so many places to choose from, of course, but we have to start somewhere.'

Emily smiled up quickly. 'It'll be great to have some-one…to have *you*,' she amended, 'to make the decision for me. I'm only just getting used to being totally independent in strange places, to try and find my own way around. And, although it's getting easier, sometimes it can be…uncomfortable.' She didn't add that she frequently felt very homesick and wished that she was back in the comparative solitude and safety of the art gallery. But she'd made the decision to spread her wings, to search life out instead of waiting for it to find her—and you didn't do that by hiding away in the cool, protective atmosphere of an art gallery.

When they arrived at the restaurant, Emily knew straight away that she was going to love it. It was on the top floor of the Hotel Hassler Roma and, as they were shown to a table by the window, soft piano music started to play quietly. Giovanni held out a chair for Emily to sit down and she glanced up at him appreciatively.

'This is…lovely, Giovanni,' she said, her eyes moist and shining with unaffected pleasure.

He returned her glance, his seductive lips parted in a brief smile. 'I had a feeling it would be right for you, Emily,' he murmured, pausing for a moment with his hand resting lightly on her bare shoulder, and she shivered instinctively.

'You're not cold?' he enquired, moving away to sit down opposite her. 'You haven't brought a wrap with you?'

'No—no, I'm not cold! It's…I'm just excited to be here,' she said quickly.

He looked across at her thoughtfully. The gentle light from the single candle on the table seemed to enhance the delicate curve of her cheek, accentuating the length of her dark eyelashes. He picked up his copy of the menu which the waiter had just given them, trying to concentrate on the selection of dishes on offer.

'You've obviously been here before, Giovanni,' Emily said with her eyes on her own menu. 'What do you recommend amongst all this?'

'I can recommend just about everything,' he said at once, 'but it depends on what you feel like.'

After a few moments, Emily put down her menu. 'I've made my decision,' she said lightly. 'I've decided that you can order for both of us.' She paused. 'And I shall trust your choice unequivocally.'

He shrugged, grinning across at her. 'Well, if you're going to live dangerously, here goes,' he said. 'And anyway, in all matters, large or small, I like to think that any woman is perfectly safe in my hands.'

Just then, the waiter came to their table and, as Giovanni

gave their order for wine, Emily gazed out of the window, swaying her shoulders lightly to the rhythm of the popular medley the pianist was playing. The hotel was situated at a spot overlooking the Spanish Steps, affording a bird's eye view of the mellow roofs of old Rome, and Emily felt grateful, again, for having met Giovanni—because he was right. She would probably have never come across this charming restaurant, and at this moment, with stars beginning to pin-prick the darkening night sky outside, and the soft lighting and friendly atmosphere in the candlelit room, Emily felt as if she had been transported to an enchanted island. And she didn't want to be rescued from it—not just yet!

Giovanni broke into her reverie. 'I've ordered white wine, Emily,' he said, 'and for the meal, I thought grilled tuna with tomatoes and taggia olives, followed by suckling pig in sweet milk sounded about right. Plus a mixed salad.' He paused. 'I hope you approve.'

'Heartily.' Emily smiled.

'And we'll consider dessert later,' Giovanni went on as the waiter departed. 'Their chocolate mousse with hot chocolate sauce is a known favourite,' he added.

'Well, if I've room, that will certainly be the one for me,' Emily said lightly, and he grinned.

'I thought so,' he said. 'That's why I mentioned it.'

Emily kept her eyes lowered for a moment. If he thought he knew her so well, she'd better watch what she said in future. This man seemed able to infiltrate her persona without even trying. He was getting close—dangerously close—she thought. But…she'd relax and enjoy it—just for tonight. There was no harm in accepting the fact that she was liking the feelings which Giovanni was arousing in her—the sense that she was not only liked, but that she was desired. And, in any case, these trifling few days would soon pass into history and would simply come in the category of harmless holiday meetings which never came to anything—and which never meant anything. Which was exactly how she wanted it. This time tomorrow she'd be back in the flat—alone—because Coral was going to spend the weekend with her parents, with just the unpacking and the laundry to fill her thoughts.

Their wine arrived and Giovanni raised his glass. 'Let's drink to…let's drink to this evening,' he murmured.

Emily picked up her own glass and gently clinked it against his. 'To this evening,' she replied slowly, letting the sparkling bubbles tease her lips and tongue. 'This is wonderful,' she added.

When the food arrived, Emily looked down at her plate. 'This is rather…generous…,' she said. 'I hope I can manage it all.'

'Do your best,' Giovanni said as he unfolded his napkin. 'You look to me as if you need just a little building up, Emily.'

But he didn't mean that, and shouldn't have said it, he thought as he watched her for a second. It was true that she had a slender figure—unlike many of his compatriots, who were more generously endowed, but she possessed the most exquisite curves and, in his experienced opinion, they were all in the right places!

Presently, he said, 'So, where are they sending you next, Emily?'

Emily picked up her glass to take a sip of wine. 'I'm not sure,' she replied. 'I shall know when I go back to work on Monday. But I normally spend the following week in the office after I've been away—to report back.' She picked up her knife and fork again. 'What about you,

Giovanni? When do you expect to leave Rome?' As soon as she'd said that, Emily wished that she hadn't because it looked as if she was trying to find out when he'd be in London.

'Oh, well, that's largely up to me,' he said casually. 'But I'll probably be there in the next week or so.' He leaned across to top up her glass. 'I have a flat in London, so I can come and go as I please.'

Hmm, Emily thought. A flat in London, and he'd said he'd a flat here in Rome too—all the education he spoke of had obviously provided him with a very sound income! She would find it difficult to be able to afford a flat of her own—sharing the rent and expenses with Coral was the only way it could work for *her*.

At that moment her mobile rang and, frowning, Emily reached into her bag to answer it. She hoped it wasn't Coral to say she'd landed herself in some sort of fix!

It wasn't Coral—it was Paul. And Emily smiled involuntarily at the sound of her brother's voice.

'Hi, Emmy,' Paul said. 'Just checking up—you're due home tomorrow, aren't you?'

'Paul! How good to hear you,' Emily said, smiling across at Giovanni briefly.

'Has it all gone well?' Paul wanted to know. 'Found your way around OK? Where are you now?'

'Everything's gone like…like a dream,' Emily said, 'and I'm sitting in a lovely restaurant having the most fabulous meal…'

'Is Coral there? Let me have a word,' Paul said. He and Coral had always got on well.

'Oh…well…Coral's not with me,' Emily said casually. 'We've sort of…parted company, just for this evening…'

'Oh? You're on your own?'

'No—not exactly…I'm having dinner with…with a friend.'

There was silence for a second. 'Someone you know?'

'Well, I do now.' Emily smiled, looking across at Giovanni again. She wished Paul wouldn't worry about her like this. 'I've met Giovanni…Giovanni Boselli,' she said hurriedly, 'and Giovanni has been a great help in finding me a couple of places I couldn't locate, and now we're enjoying a fantastic meal, Paul… I must bring you here one day.'

She could just imagine the expression on Paul's face. Where his sister was concerned, he saw predatory males on every corner.

'Oh…well, then,' Paul said. 'Have a good time, and safe travelling tomorrow, Emmy. I'll ring you later on…' He paused, lowering his voice. 'Take care, won't you…be *careful,* Emmy.' Then, 'Dad sends his love, by the way.'

They ended the call and Emily replaced the phone in her bag, not looking at Giovanni, but she knew he hadn't taken his eyes off her. She decided not to tell him that Paul was her brother. Let him think what he liked. And, for a ridiculous moment, Giovanni felt a surge of jealousy run through him at the way Emily's eyes had lit up as she'd spoken to the man at the other end. It had to mean that it was someone special…even though she'd said she wasn't in a relationship at the moment.

By the time they'd finished the meal—with neither of them having the chocolate mousse—it was almost midnight, and reluctantly they left the restaurant and began strolling back to where Giovanni had parked his car. Emily sighed, taking a deep breath as she looked up at the sky.

'This evening has been the perfect way to end my tour,' she said. 'Thank you, Giovanni.'

'I consider it to have been a…privilege to have your company, Emily,' he replied, and there was no teasing note in his voice as he said it.

What happened in the next couple of seconds would always remain a blur in Emily's memory—but, without any warning at all, her ankle suddenly twisted horribly and with surprising force—so that she found herself sprawling to the ground, her arms flailing helplessly at something, anything, to help her. And, although Giovanni had been walking very close beside her, he was not able to do a thing to stop her falling. Then, with an incoherent curse, he sprang forward and grabbed hold of her and pulled her to her feet.

With a gasp of unbelievable pain, Emily tried to put her foot to the ground, but could only lean against him as he held her in a tight, protective embrace. *'Oh,'* she said, gritting her teeth to stop from shrieking aloud, 'what on *earth* did I trip over?'

Still holding her, he glanced down at the pavement. 'Well, these slabs are very uneven—look at that one— that's what you must have caught your foot on.' He looked down at her, resting his chin on her head for a second. 'How…how bad do you think it is, Emily? Can you put any weight on it?'

Now her ankle was throbbing with hammer blows and, for a terrible moment, Emily felt her head swimming. She hoped she wasn't going to disgrace herself and faint in public! 'This has happened to me before,' she admitted. 'Perhaps I've weakened this ankle, so I'll have to be more careful in future.' With her full weight against him for support, she looked up into his eyes and, even in the dim mellowness of the street lighting, he could see that her face was ashen.

'Come on,' he said. 'We're very close to my flat. You need to sit down for a few minutes and recover.' With his arm firmly around her waist, he almost carried Emily the length of the street and around the corner. Half hopping, half walking, Emily was in no position to suggest any alternative, and in a couple of minutes they reached an ancient stone archway through which she could see a discreet block of shuttered dwellings.

'Mine's on the ground floor,' Giovanni said, 'so there are no steps to negotiate.'

Although the building was unprepossessing from the outside, inside it was a different matter. Giovanni gently guided Emily across the large tile-floored sitting room to lie her down on an elegant chaise longue.

'There, keep your feet up for a few minutes and let's see what you've done to yourself,' he said.

As he switched on the numerous table lamps, the room was immediately swathed in a gentle, soothing glow and, in spite of feeling extremely shaky, Emily couldn't help admiring her surroundings. It was a cool, comfortable room and clearly very expensively furnished.

He came over and knelt down beside her, not removing her sandal but taking her ankle very carefully in his warm hands. 'Can you move it about, Emily?' he asked. 'Try to turn it—very gently—from side to side.' He peered at it more closely. 'It does look rather swollen,' he added.

Emily did as she was told. 'Well, I'm sure it's not broken,' she said, 'and, as I said, this has happened before. I think I've probably just sprained it again, that's all.' She looked at him ruefully. 'Sorry to be such a pain, Giovanni…'

'Wasn't your fault,' he said. 'That could happen to anybody.' He massaged her foot gently for a few moments, smoothing it rhythmically with the palms of both hands.

'It does feel hot,' he said. He stood up and looked down into her upturned face, relieved to see that some colour had returned to her cheeks. 'I'll get an ice pack from the fridge to put on it…and would you like a glass of water—or anything else?' he asked.

She smiled up. 'Yes—some water, please,' she said, thankful that her heart rate had lessened and that the feeling of dizziness had passed.

Left by herself for a few moments, Emily had a good look around her. It was quite obviously a man's abode, she thought, having very few frills or ornaments—apart from several framed photographs displayed on a large mahogany cabinet. There was one of two little girls in swimsuits on a beach somewhere, and someone else crouching and hugging a dog around its neck, but in the front was one of a beautiful dark-eyed girl with a generous smile. She was obviously someone rather special, Emily thought—no doubt one of Giovanni's many girlfriends… Then her gaze flickered to a smaller one of Giovanni with his arm held protectively around the shoulders of the same girl, who was looking up at him adoringly.

Just then Giovanni returned and Emily sipped gratefully from the glass of water he handed her, leaning forward slightly to watch him as he placed the ice pack, which he'd wrapped in a small towel, around her foot.

'This will help,' he said, supporting it in place with two cushions. 'And presently I'll go and fetch the car and take you back to the hotel.' He paused. 'Do you have an early start tomorrow? What time's your flight?'

'Two p.m., if I remember rightly,' Emily replied, feeling suddenly as if she were in a dream. The whole day had turned out so unexpectedly, she thought…and being with Giovanni for so much of it was the most unexpected thing of all. But she knew that she'd enjoyed every minute of it, had enjoyed being with this—all right, say it, she told herself—being with this heart-throb of masculinity. And even now, being here with him in his flat, was rather un-believable. It was certainly nothing which she could have anticipated.

He was still kneeling on the floor beside her, pressing the ice pack more firmly against her foot now and then, and looking up at her occasionally with that special sensuous smile which Emily was getting used to, and which had the effect of sending delicious shivers down her spine. She looked over his shoulder, nodding at the pho-tographs on display. 'Are you fond of photography?' she asked casually, hoping he'd tell her who all the people were in the pictures. Tell her who that girl was.

'Oh—off and on,' he replied non-committally. 'I'm not someone who likes to snap away at everything in sight and clutter up my home with hundreds of albums, that's for sure.' He leaned back slightly. 'But it's my mother who's snap-happy. She keeps giving me fresh ones to put on show.'

Emily glanced up at him quickly as he spoke. Something in his tone, something in the unusually dark expression flickering across his features made her wish she hadn't shown any interest in his belongings. He'd already inti-mated that there was some friction somewhere in the family…

And Giovanni, acutely aware of Emily's vulnerable presence so near to him, couldn't help thinking how ironic the situation was. She was a beautiful woman, he enjoyed her company, enjoyed everything about her, had already imagined what it would be like to make love to her—and here she was, lying on his sofa with a sprained ankle!

How different it might have been if he could have invited her here for an intimate meal, if they could have talked long into the night, and then, later, much later, from the comfort of his king-size bed, could have watched the dawn break together. Some hopes!

After a while, Emily slid off the chaise longue and gingerly tried putting her foot to the floor—and, thankfully, Giovanni's treatment had worked like a miracle.

'It's fine now—really,' she said, looking up at him. 'Thank you, Dr Giovanni. I'll be OK now.'

He had got to his feet, still holding her protectively around the waist, then stood back. 'That's good—you stay right here and I'll fetch the car,' he said.

While he was gone, Emily limped over to the cabinet and peered closely at the girl in the picture. Her facial expression was so lively that Emily felt she could discern what the girl was thinking when that shot was taken. Whoever she was, Emily thought, she was a living part of this room. A presence. No wonder she had pride of place, right there in front of all the others.

Emily turned away, shrugging slightly. So what? What did it matter to her, anyway?

# CHAPTER FOUR

'WELL, *you've* certainly made a night of it!' Coral exclaimed. 'Do you realize what the time is—I was beginning to get worried,' she teased.

Coral was sitting up in bed, half dozing, half reading, but now that Emily had returned she soon became fully awake and ready for a long chat. 'Come on,' she said. 'Where did you go…and was the sumptuous Giovanni good company—or shouldn't I ask?'

At this point Emily wished with all her heart that she had her own room, rather than sharing. She definitely did not feel like giving Coral a blow-by-blow account of the last few hours. But she knew she wasn't going to be let off easily.

'Oh—we had dinner in a lovely restaurant,' she said casually, 'and there was a pianist playing all my favourite numbers.' She went across to the bathroom. 'But how about you? Did Nico come up to expectations?'

Coral couldn't wait to pour out all the details. 'Ellie, he is just *gorgeous!* We strolled all around the city—to places you and I haven't been to—and we stopped by the Trevi Fountain and I threw a coin in and made a wish! Then we sat outside at a small restaurant and had a nice meal—nothing too extravagant, of course, because I don't think he's rich or anything, but Emmy he was so…so…special. So attentive. Made me feel like a princess,' she added somewhat wistfully. 'I mean, Steve never treated me like that, ever—but Nico, *he* did, and he was so charming… wanted to know all about me, what I did, where I lived.' She paused for breath. 'And, guess what—he's going to come to England—maybe next month, especially to see me! What do you think of that?' She flopped back on her pillow. 'I never dreamed for a second that I'd meet someone—anyone—who could make me feel so…so…romantic.' She looked up at Emily. 'I think I'm in love. Do you think I'm mad?'

'Yes,' Emily replied, going into the bathroom and shutting the door firmly.

She switched on the shower and stood under the rush of warm water for several moments before beginning to soap herself gently. Coral was so—so—*suggestible,* she thought, so ready to read something into nothing. Of course, Nico seemed a nice enough man, but he was young—significantly younger than Coral—and he was obviously cutting his emotional teeth on this impressionable Englishwoman—and she would not have been the first, either. And now Coral was letting herself believe that she was about to have the grand love affair! Honestly!

Emily stepped out of the shower and started towelling herself briskly, feeling distinctly rattled. Suddenly, she didn't want to be here. Then she paused, glancing at herself in the mirror as she rubbed gently at her soaking wet hair. She knew very well why she was feeling suddenly miserable and deflated. And it was nothing to do with Coral's enthusiastic and immature reactions, either. It was everything to do with Signor Giovanni Boselli—how could she have allowed him to get to her so easily, to engender feelings in her that she thought she had got well under control? Emily realized how easily she had fallen under his spell—the dangerous spell of a handsome Italian who was obviously well practised at flattering the opposite sex. He'd certainly made her feel special—as no doubt he'd done with that girl in the photograph. And plenty of others like her.

She took her gown from the hook on the door and went back into the bedroom. Coral was still awake and Emily knew that there'd have to be more lively chat before sleep was allowed. Reaching for the hairdryer, she tried to smile brightly.

'So—has Nico been to the UK before?' she asked. 'Does he know anyone over there?'

'Not a soul,' Coral said, 'so I said he could stay with us—it would only be for a week or so, Ellie.'

Emily made a face. 'Coral—you shouldn't be quite so free with your invites,' she said. 'We only have the extra sofa bed in the sitting room, remember.'

'I told him that, and he said that would be great.' Coral sighed. 'He's going to teach me Italian,' she said. 'That's what we were doing over dinner. I've learned a few phrases already.' She sat up, drawing her knees to her chin. 'Now, tell me more about Giovanni... I can't believe that my evening was more exciting than yours.'

Emily filled in a few details, describing the moment that she'd fallen down, but when she went on to say that she'd been to Giovanni's flat, that was something else!

'You went to his place? Ellie! No wonder you were a bit slow telling me that! What was it like—and what was *he* like?'

'I have no idea what you're implying,' Emily said loftily, 'but his flat is in a luxury block—and it was quite sparsely furnished, but all obviously very well planned and very expensive.' She paused. 'And the only human contact we had while I was there was when he continued pressing a huge ice pack on my foot. *Very* romantic,' she said sarcastically.

'That was bad luck—you twisting that ankle again, Ellie,' Coral said seriously. 'It's about the third time you've done that lately, isn't it…and *next* time the gorgeous Giovanni may not be there to rescue you!'

They had plenty of time to spare the next morning, so after a leisurely breakfast Emily and Coral packed their belongings and went down to the hall to await the taxi which would take them to the airport.

'It's Nico's day off today,' Coral said, glancing across at the reception desk, which was being manned by yet another good-looking Italian. 'Where do they *get* all these men?' she added, lowering her voice. 'Just look at *him*!'

Emily sighed. 'I think it's high time we got back to London and reality,' she said. But she was relieved to find that this morning she herself felt more grounded, more normal. She realized that being away from home, with sunshine and good food and wine, could all be a heady combination and, although it would be a long time before she'd forget Giovanni's mesmerizing gaze, today she was totally in control once more. Today she wasn't experiencing those ridiculous schoolgirl feelings that she'd felt last night… The only physical hurt that remained was a slight twinge in her ankle now and then. Just enough to make her careful where she walked.

They arrived at the airport in good time and after they'd checked in Coral announced that she was going to use the Ladies' room.

This was not nearly so crowded a place as Heathrow, Emily thought as she stared around her—and the gathering queues seemed to be mostly holidaymakers. Glancing up at the monitors, she saw that their flight number had not yet been announced—but there was plenty of time, she thought idly.

Suddenly, to her total astonishment, she saw Giovanni. He was standing at the far end of the hall looking around him, and for a few seconds Emily didn't get up from her seat, aware that her heart was fluttering madly again... Well, he had to be the most fantastically attractive man in the building—in the universe, she could have added—so why wouldn't any woman's heart beat just that little bit faster? And how did he always manage to look so elegant—even in casual clothes?

She got up then and walked across to him slowly. He spotted her almost immediately and his face broke into a wide grin as he quickened his pace to come and stand by her side. He was holding an elegant spray of red roses. Emily was the first to speak.

'Giovanni...' she began, trying not to sound breathless. 'What...what are *you* doing here?' she said, though the answer was pretty obvious. The way he was looking down at her spoke volumes.

'I just had to see how you were today, Emilee-a,' he replied easily. He wasn't going to say that he'd lain awake most of the night, thinking about her. Wanting her. He put his hand lightly on her shoulder. 'Your ankle... I was worried that this morning it would not be good—that you might have difficulty walking.' He paused, then handed her the flowers. 'For you,' he said simply. 'To say sorry.'

Emily took the flowers from him, then bent her head to smell them. They were fragrant and perfectly shaped.

She looked up at Giovanni. 'To say sorry? What for, Giovanni?' she asked.

'I felt responsible, Emily,' he said. 'You trusted yourself to my care last night, and I should have spotted that loose stone...I should have prevented you from falling.'

Emily smiled up at him. 'Of course you shouldn't, Giovanni, it was my own silly fault,' she said quickly. 'I told you, it's happened before. You'd think I'd be more careful!' She looked down at the roses again. 'But I can't say I'm sorry that you've brought me these beautiful roses! Thank you—thank you so much, Giovanni. They're lovely.' She paused. 'But you really must not feel guilty. I should have looked where I was going.'

Although she hadn't imagined for a moment that she would be seeing him today, Emily couldn't help feeling flattered—and excited—that he'd turned up, despite the talking-to she'd given herself earlier about the perils of being in the company of gorgeous Italians. But it was really good of him to be so considerate, she thought. And, anyway, he was only being kind.

Just then Coral appeared, and when she saw the pair standing together, her reaction was fairly predictable. 'Goodness me...Gio...' she began, her eyes wide, and Emily cut in quickly.

'Giovanni was worried that I might be crippled this morning,' she said, 'so he just looked in to make sure I was...everything was...OK. Wasn't that thoughtful of him?'

'*Very* thoughtful,' Coral said, her interested gaze going from one to the other with unashamed interest. 'Don't worry, Gio,' she said, 'I'll make sure that Ellie gets home safe and sound.'

Giovanni looked down at Coral with his usual disarming smile.

Presently, it was time for them to go through to the departure lounge, and for Giovanni to take his leave.

'Safe travelling,' he murmured, his gaze lingering on Emily's upturned face. 'I'll...be in touch, Emilee-a,' he added softly.

'Goodbye, Giovanni,' she said, 'and thank you so much...again.'

Then he turned and walked rapidly away without a backward glance, and Coral stared at his retreating back. 'What a yummy Italian,' she said sadly. 'You've made a hit there, Ellie. He couldn't take his eyes off you.'

'Rubbish,' Emily said. 'He's just that sort... He was really concerned about me falling down last night, felt it was all his fault. That's the only reason he bothered to find me today. Just to make sure.'

When they got back home, Coral left for her parents' house and Emily took Giovanni's card from her bag and dialled his mobile phone number. Well, it was only polite... They'd barely had chance to say goodbye properly. He answered almost immediately and when he heard who was calling he said, 'Ah...Emilee-e-a,' with just that lingering intonation at the end of her name which had the familiar effect of making her knees feel slightly shaky.

'Giovanni,' she said quickly. 'I thought...I thought you'd like to know that we got home safely but really I want to thank you again for the roses... They are absolutely lovely. You shouldn't have spoiled me like that. But thank you so much... What have I done to deserve them?'

There was a moment's hesitation before he answered. 'All beautiful women deserve to be spoiled,' he said easily, and Emily shook her head briefly. She wondered how many times he'd used that one before.

He cleared his throat. 'I'm glad you called, Emily, because I've just heard that I need to be in the UK next week—just for a few days. It would be good to see you,' he added.

Emily bit her lip. This felt all wrong—it *was* wrong—and she knew it. During the flight home, she'd made up her mind that she wasn't letting this—association—with Giovanni go any further. It wasn't that she didn't trust him as a person—it was more to do with not trusting herself, and relationships in general. The problem was, he'd said he sometimes came to the UK so it was obvious that they'd meet up—something told her he'd make sure of that! And each time they did would make it more difficult…difficult to refuse to see him, and even more difficult to deny herself the pleasure! And, in any case, with the choice of women he so obviously would have, she'd soon slip down his list of priorities. No, thanks, she wasn't going down that road again, she thought firmly.

She waited before answering, trying to find the right words. She'd so enjoyed herself yesterday evening—the meal, the atmosphere in the restaurant, the slow stroll afterwards—even if it had ended rather dramatically. And she remembered all too clearly the feel of his arms around her, holding her so protectively after she'd fallen, remembered the feel of his hands, warm and consoling as he'd massaged her ankle in that firm but gentle caress. She cleared her throat.

'It's been really great to have met you, to have known you, Giovanni,' she said, adding softly, 'I've…enjoyed it. But I'm going to be very busy at work next week, so I don't think we'll be able to meet up. Sorry.'

Giovanni grinned to himself. He knew a rebuttal when he met it.

'No worries,' he said easily. 'I understand.' And, after chatting for a few more minutes, they finished the call and he rang off. And Emily sat where she was for several moments, staring at the phone. Well, that was easy enough, she thought. He had accepted her very firm refusal to see him again with no attempt to make her change her mind. He hadn't even bothered to prolong their conversation, keeping it short and sweet. She shrugged. Oh, well, it had been an experience, being with him for that brief interlude.

Standing by the window in his flat, a slow smile spread over Giovanni's dark features. The challenge ahead excited him. So, Signorina Emily was going to give him a run for his money, was she? Give him a hard time. But he was up for it, and he knew he'd win in the end. She liked him—he was sure of that—even fancied him, just a little. So he'd have to work hard at heightening any feelings she already had for him, until they burned with the same passion that he admitted, quite unashamedly, he had felt for her from the very first moment they'd met at the shop. She had seemed to light up the space around her with a kind of magic...and he'd wanted to be close enough to her to share in it. And he still felt exactly the same now—nothing had changed. But maybe *he* was changing, he thought, thanks to almost six months of complete rest from all the pressures, all the hurt that had weighed him down so relentlessly.

He bit his lip thoughtfully. He would be in England next week, he knew where Emily worked, and now he had her phone number. And, however busy she said she was, she'd make time for him. In his mind, there was no doubt about that!

He went across to the cabinet and poured himself a drink. 'To us, Emilee-a,' he murmured, raising his glass. 'To you and me. And Lady Luck.'

# CHAPTER FIVE

'You *can't* turn me down tonight, Emily,' Justin said softly. 'Not on my birthday!'

Emily looked up quickly, trying not to look as irritated as she felt. Justin simply would not take no for an answer—and it was beginning to get on her nerves. What made it worse was that they were always seated next to each other, so he was a constant presence in the busy upstairs office. Not to mention the fact that he happened to be the boss's son—which made it doubly awkward for her to keep turning him down. But, the fact was, she didn't fancy him, not one bit, and didn't relish the thought of them being alone together off duty.

'But how much more celebrating do you need to do, Justin?' she said, giving him a rather watery smile. The entire staff had already been to a wine bar at lunchtime to honour the occasion, and someone had bought cream cakes to go with the afternoon cup of tea.

Justin gazed down at her thoughtfully. He couldn't understand her reticence. He'd tried so many times to get her to accept his offer of a night out somewhere, and he'd certainly never been turned down by anyone before. But Emily was different from all the others…and, as far as he knew, she hadn't been out with anyone else from work, either. He frowned slightly as he looked down at her. She always looked so fantastic in the regulation black suit and white shirt, her sheer black tights and high-heeled shoes doing full justice to her slim legs and dainty feet.

'Well, it's just that we might round off the day in spectacular fashion,' he said, a slightly teasing note in his voice. 'Make it one to really remember.'

Emily turned her attention back to her computer. She had made up her mind that she was not going with him anywhere tonight, but neither did she want to offend. He was a nice enough bloke, but his persistence was becoming over-familiar and she'd had enough of it.

'I'm sure you've a whole list of suitable partners to make your dreams come true tonight, Justin,' she said, 'but I'm already spoken for, I'm afraid.' She shifted some papers on her desk. 'I'm entertaining someone to dinner at home tonight—a long-standing arrangement which I can't possibly alter.'

He waited a moment before replying. Then, 'I don't believe you,' he said teasingly—but meaning it.

Emily felt really angry at that. How dared the man doubt her honesty? But it was too late—she'd told a lie and now she'd have to brave it out. 'Believe what you like,' she said flatly, her colour rising. 'The fact remains that I'm not free to accept your kind offer and, before I even begin to think about tonight, I've got all these lists to complete, so if you don't mind…'

As it happened, it had been an exceptionally busy day for everyone, and it was gone seven o'clock before all the staff finally left the office, spilling out onto the pavement and making their 'goodnights' to each other.

'What have you got lined up for this evening, Justin?' one of the other men asked. 'Something special?'

'It was going to be special,' Justin said breezily, glancing at Emily, 'but I've been turned down. Still, I shan't be spending it alone, I promise you.'

Everyone then went their separate ways and, to Emily's annoyance, Justin fell into step beside her as she began to walk away.

Then, from a doorway close in front of them, a dark voice suddenly uttered her name and Emily could have shrieked in amazement—and delight!

'Giovanni!' she cried and, without a moment's hesitation, she almost threw herself at him, clutching him around the neck and offering him her mouth to be kissed. And Giovanni, momentarily transfixed by her reception, wasted no time in closing his lips over hers—putting his arms around her waist and lifting her right off her feet.

'Emilee-a,' he began, putting her down gently but before he could say anything more, she cut in.

'Giovanni, this is Justin—who happens to work with me,' and, turning now to Justin, she said triumphantly, 'and this, Justin, is Giovanni Boselli.'

To give him his due, Justin managed not to look too taken aback at what he'd just witnessed—he'd never realized that Emily could express herself so...so freely, like that—and he cleared his throat.

'Good to meet you...Giovanni...' he muttered. 'So, you're the lady's choice, then, are you...? Well, I do hope that you have a pleasant evening with Emily.' He paused. 'I've heard that she's a fair cook, so I'm sure she won't disappoint you tonight.'

It hadn't taken long for Giovanni to size up the situation, and he made good use of it, his arms still wound around Emily's waist. He'd wondered what sort of greeting he'd get from her, because she'd had no idea that he was going to turn up—he'd decided to surprise her rather than give her time to think up an excuse. And it seemed to have worked better than he could have dreamed!

'Emily has never disappointed me in anything,' he murmured, smiling down into her upturned face, his eyes twinkling mischievously.

'Well, have a great evening,' Justin said. 'See you on Monday, Emily.'

As soon as he'd gone, Emily disentangled herself from Giovanni, who made no effort to stop her, merely grinning down at her.

'I had no idea that you'd missed me so much, Emily,' he said smoothly. Then, more seriously, 'I take it that I was a useful, shall we say, decoy just now?'

Emily glanced up at him rather shamefacedly as they began to walk towards the tube station, thinking how suave he was looking in his dark business suit and grey shirt, though the loosened tie around his neck hung down casually 'Yes, sorry if I embarrassed you, Giovanni,' she said. 'But I refused to go out with Justin this evening, even though it is his birthday, saying that I was entertaining someone at home tonight. And he didn't believe me—quite rightly, I'm afraid. But, when I saw you there, I was able to…well…play the part, shall we say. It was as if fate had stepped in to make things easy for me!'

'I'm always very…happy…to be of service,' he said softly, putting his arm through hers protectively and his touch—now that they were alone—made Emily's breasts tingle. She quickened her step.

'How did you know that I'd be around, anyway?' she

asked, not looking up at him. 'I didn't tell you where I worked...'

'I knew the firm, but not the branch office,' he said, 'so I took a chance and looked in earlier this afternoon and asked if Emily Sinclair was in today—and the girl on the desk told me what I needed to know. My own office is only a ten minute walk away, where I've had to be for the last few days, so it was no big deal. And, if you hadn't worked there, I'd have tried the other branches until I found you,' he added.

After a moment, Emily said, 'You could have rung me first.'

'What—to have you turn me down?' he said, that teasing note in his voice again. 'No chance!' He took her elbow more firmly, to steer her across the road. 'And now that I am here, you have no choice but to be my date for the evening. I've several suggestions where we might go.'

Emily's emotions were totally mixed up now. She freely admitted that she'd felt absolutely blown away to see Giovanni standing there—it couldn't have worked better for her to convince Justin that she was spoken for that evening—but it wasn't only that. She knew that the very sight of Giovanni had set her heart pounding. In the intervening days since they'd been together she'd hardly stopped thinking about him, and to see him again in the all-too-seductive flesh had set her senses spinning. Which was why she hadn't wanted to meet him again—if she could help it. He was threatening to thwart her plans to remain emotionally uninvolved with anyone at all—at least for the foreseeable future. *Remember Marcus,* she kept telling herself, *remember how you felt when he decided he didn't want you any more, that he loved someone else. Can you bear the thought of that happening all over again?* But Emily knew with a sinking heart that every time she was near to Giovanni it would be increasingly difficult to resist him, and it wasn't her fault that he'd turned up tonight. So she'd have to deal with it as best she could.

Pulling herself away from all these thoughts, she glanced up at him as they joined the teeming home-going masses on the Underground. 'Well, I think I owe you one, Giovanni,' she said. 'A meal, I mean,' she added hurriedly. 'If you think you can trust my cooking, I'd be happy do the honours this evening.' She paused. 'I am rather tired, as a matter of fact—it's been a long week, and going out anywhere doesn't really appeal.'

'Sounds perfect to me,' he murmured. 'I hope Coral won't mind my intruding on her space.'

'Oh, Coral won't be there,' Emily said. 'She's staying at her parents' home in North Wales. She'll be back on Sunday night.' She didn't look at Giovanni as she spoke. She was going to make it very clear at the outset that she was merely being polite and returning his generosity by providing him with supper. It wouldn't be quite up to the standard of the meal they'd had in Rome, but her reputation in the culinary stakes was fairly high. She was the one who usually cooked when she and Coral were together at home.

The flat which the two girls shared was in a quiet residential street in a suburb of the city and, as she opened the front door, Emily glanced up at Giovanni.

'I'm afraid our place isn't quite as grand as yours,' she said lightly. 'Not so big, anyway,' she added.

He followed her up to the first floor, and as they entered the flat he looked around him appreciatively. 'It's very nice, Emily,' he murmured. 'Perfect for two working girls, I should have thought.'

As Emily had said, it was not large, only boasting a

sitting room, two small bedrooms, a minute galley of a kitchen and a bathroom with only enough space to accommodate the usual facilities and a shower cubicle.

'I shall own my own place one day,' Emily said, 'but this will do for the moment—and sharing the rent and all the expenses with Coral means that I can save up.' She smiled at Giovanni, who stood with his hands in his pockets, glancing around him.

'It's a very…pretty…home,' he said. He looked down at her. 'Just the sort of place I'd imagine you to be living in, Emily.'

His speculative eye had noted the expensive curtains at the windows, the luxurious cushions scattered around and the framed pictures on the wall, three of which were graced with soft over-lighting. He went closer to inspect them, his eyes narrowing. They were all watercolours, mostly of charming pastoral scenes, with one seascape and a couple of still life.

'I don't recognize any of these paintings,' he said, turning to look down at her.

'No,' she said, 'because they're originals.' She paused. 'They're my own feeble efforts, I'm afraid.'

Giovanni was genuinely amazed—and impressed. He knew a good painting when he saw one, and these were, to his mind, professionally done. But then he remembered that she'd said she'd worked in an art gallery, so it was obviously a subject dear to her heart. 'They are not feeble—they are fantastic, Emilee-a,' he said slowly. 'You have a real gift.' He looked back at the pictures for a moment. 'But you must know that, without me pointing it out, surely? What on earth are you doing in a travel agency?'

'I did do an Arts degree at university,' she said, 'and I'm never happier than when I've got a paintbrush in my hand.

But I'd have to be exceptionally good—and very lucky—to earn my living at it, so I work where someone will pay me.' She turned away. 'Maybe one day I'll be able to afford to just sit at my easel and paint…but goodness only knows whether that'll ever happen. I'd need a fairy godmother—or a big win on the Lottery, which I don't do, in any case.'

'Your family—your father—must think you're brilliant,' Giovanni said, still staring at the pictures.

Emily smiled. 'Yes, I suppose he does,' she said. 'But he would, because I'm his daughter. All parents think their kids are brilliant, don't they? And that's not a good enough recommendation. He insisted on rigging up those lights, and he's done the same for a few of the ones I've given him at home,' she added.

'Well, I'd recommend your expertise any day,' Giovanni said firmly—and meant it. 'Haven't you tried selling any?'

'I'd be too embarrassed to try!' Emily said at once. 'I'd only have to be rejected once, and that would be it! So I restrict myself to giving them away as presents to friends.'

'I hope that I come into that category,' Giovanni said, 'because I'd love one of your paintings, Emily—for my flat.' He turned to glance at her. 'And I'd be happy to pay your price—whatever it was.' He paused, looking straight into her eyes. 'Feasting one's eyes on beautiful things cheers you up,' he added. 'It's good for the soul.'

Emily suddenly felt almost overcome by all this flattery and she said quickly, 'Look, I must just change out of my work clothes, then I'll start getting our dinner. Make yourself at home, Giovanni.' She switched on the television, handing him the remote control. 'And help yourself to something from our rather modest drinks table,' she said as she went into her bedroom.

Doing as he was told, Giovanni poured himself a small whisky, then wandered over to the window thoughtfully. He was quietly amazed at how things had turned out today—amazed that he'd been able to track Emily down so easily, and gobsmacked when she'd thrown her arms around his neck in the street like that—although the reason for that had been made very clear straight away. He smiled to himself. Thanks, Justin, he thought. If it wasn't for you, I mightn't be here at all, now. He took a drink from his glass. Just another piece of luck which had come his way so unexpectedly.

Sitting down on the sofa, he switched on the TV, flicking through the channels for a few moments, and presently Emily emerged, wearing tight jeans and a white T-shirt, her hair brushed out loosely around her shoulders. She seemed to have removed her make-up, he noticed, as he admired the natural, fresh glow of her skin, and he stood up immediately, deciding not to compliment her on her appearance, even though it was the first thing he would normally do with any female he happened to be with. And most of them responded to it very happily. But he knew he had to tread carefully where this woman was concerned… She seemed to have her feet very firmly on the ground, and wouldn't necessarily appreciate too much sweet-talk.

'It won't take me too long to get our food,' she said lightly, 'so do freshen up while I do it, Giovanni—if you want to.' She smiled, indicating the bathroom. 'You don't need a map to find your way around our flat.' She turned to go into the kitchen, saying over her shoulder, 'My brother was supposed to be spending the evening with me—but he hasn't been very well for the past few days so was going to go straight home to bed. And I always plan something a bit special when he eats here with me, so I hope you'll approve of tonight's menu.'

Giovanni grinned. 'There won't be any trouble on that score, Emily,' he said. 'Especially as I only had a very quick bite with the others at lunchtime.'

Emily took the two generously sized veal cutlets from the fridge. She'd prepared them before leaving for work that morning, wrapping them in cheese and a fine slice of ham before coating them in breadcrumbs. They'd only take a few minutes to cook, she thought. She'd also par-boiled and sliced the potatoes, which were now ready to be layered with onion, butter and cream and baked quickly for a short time in the oven. And there'd be green veg-etables or salad—Giovanni could make that choice, she thought.

She smiled as she busied herself. She did love entertain-ing—not that she did very much of it now. There never seemed much time, and she was often away from home in any case. But this was what she liked best—just cooking for two. Sometimes it would be for Paul or her father, very occasionally, but more often it would be just her and Coral.

She finished preparing the potatoes, popping them into the oven just as Giovanni came to stand in the doorway. Leaning casually against the wall, he said, 'This was some-thing I did not expect, Emily—to watch you beavering away on my behalf. I'd hoped to be able to buy you dinner somewhere tonight.'

She looked up at him quickly. 'But you did that when we were in Rome,' she said. 'Now it's your turn to be treated.' She paused for a moment. 'Now, would you prefer salad or green vegetables? Your choice.'

He stared down at her for a long moment, thinking that

his 'choice' wouldn't have anything to do with food. He'd glanced in at her open bedroom door as he'd gone into the bathroom—her bed looked extremely comfortable and very inviting! But he knew very well that his carnal instincts were not going to be satisfied—not here, not with Emily Sinclair. But he was an experienced lover of women, each of whom had to be treated as an individual, he knew that. No rushing in where angels fear to tread, he thought.

He cleared his throat, trying to keep his mind on food. 'Any green vegetable will be great, Emily,' he said in answer to her question.

'Good. I was hoping you'd say that,' she said lightly.

As she was fairly sure it would, the meal turned out well and Giovanni was unstinting in his praise. 'Not only does the lady paint like an angel, she also cooks like one,' he murmured, glancing across at her as they sat together at the diminutive table in the window. By now, it was getting quite dark outside. Emily had switched on the discreet lamps in the room and the effect was cosy, soothing and intimate. Giovanni, feeling relaxed and totally at ease, put down his knife and fork and looked around him. 'I imagine that the décor here is all down to you, Emily?' he asked casually.

'Mostly,' Emily replied, 'and it's a good thing that Coral is so easy-going. She never argues about anything, so she was quite happy for me to choose the material and make the curtains and the cushion covers.' She took his empty plate and began to clear the dishes. She paused for a moment, the dishes in her hand. 'There is one big matter on which we're disagreeing at the moment though,' she said. 'It's Nico… Do you remember that it was Nico who she spent the last evening with in Rome? Well, he not only turned up at the airport to see her off, but apparently he's phoned her every single day since we returned to England, stating his undying love for her, and Coral, being Coral, is falling for it!' Emily sighed. 'She keeps phoning me to give me all the details and she's so excited. I don't like to pour cold water on her enthusiasm…but honestly—can anybody be *that* gullible?'

'You obviously don't believe in love at first sight, then, Emily?' Giovanni asked mildly.

'No,' Emily replied flatly. 'Do you?'

'Yes,' he said slowly, 'I certainly do—for some people.'

Emily shrugged. 'Well, I don't think that Nico is right for Coral. Good heavens—they've only spent a few hours together! And he's much younger than her.' She turned to go into the kitchen.

After a few moments, Emily came back from the kitchen carrying a glass dish of perfect strawberries and a fondue full of melted dark chocolate. Striking a match, she lit a flame beneath it and looked across at Giovanni.

'I hope you like this pudding,' she said. 'It's my brother's favourite.'

'I don't often indulge in puddings,' Giovanni said, 'but I'm not going to turn this one down.'

There was silence for a few moments as they each dipped the succulent fruit into the piping-hot chocolate, transferring it to their mouths carefully and looking across at each other, Giovanni's eyes twinkling. There was something intrinsically sensuous about hot chocolate—hot dark chocolate—he thought as he watched Emily savouring the thickly coated strawberry she'd just put into her mouth. As she raised her eyes to look back at him, he noticed the tiniest shred of chocolate staining her cheek and, without thinking, he automatically leaned forward slowly and gently, very gently, wiped it away with his napkin, pausing with his fingers caressing her warm skin before cupping her chin in his hands. For a second they both stayed quite still, looking into each other's eyes without speaking, and Giovanni was painfully aware of his heightened pulse-rate, while Emily felt almost transfixed in her chair. The nerves in her neck were jangling, tingling, and she felt an unbelievable sensation invading the whole of her body, right down to her toes. A sensation she had never, ever experienced before, and it left her shaky and bewildered.

He sat back then, still gazing at her, and Emily looked away quickly. It was time to make some strong coffee!

'Thank you,' she said, hoping that her voice didn't sound as odd to him as it did to her. 'Dribbling chocolate all over yourself may only be done at home,' she added, trying to erase the memory of the last few moments. 'Would you like some cheese?' she enquired.

He followed her into the kitchen, wishing that his body would leave him alone. 'No, I don't want anything to take away the taste of that delicious dessert,' he said.

'Then we'll just have coffee,' Emily said.

Presently, after they'd cleared up the dishes, they went into the sitting room with the coffee things and Emily leaned forward to pour the steaming liquid into two mugs. She already knew from the other times they'd been together that Giovanni liked his black with no sugar and, as she handed him his mug, he held her gaze for a second.

'That was *the* most fantastic meal, Emily,' he said quietly. 'In fact, it has been a remarkable evening,' he added huskily, and Emily stirred cream into her mug quickly to avoid having to interpret his remark. He was sitting next to her on the sofa, but there was no bodily contact between them—for which Emily was profoundly grateful. Why was she still feeling so churned up inside? she asked herself. Giovanni Boselli had struck a nerve in her which she hadn't known existed and, although it was the most delicious sensation she'd ever experienced, it had put her on the alert, making her almost dizzy with a mixture of exhilaration and anxious desperation. It could be described as the same feeling she always had on extreme fairground rides, she thought…when she was going upwards, upwards towards a terrifying apex, then to hover tremblingly for a few seconds before being catapulted forward into a mind-blowing, breathtaking vortex—yet not really knowing how it was all going to end. She took another sip from her mug. She must not let Giovanni get to her any further, she told herself. It was all very well giving Coral good advice—she needed some herself, right now!

Later, after they'd finished their coffee, he glanced at his watch. 'I ought to be going,' he said. 'Do you realize that it's eleven-thirty?' He smiled across at her, feeling that somehow he'd crossed a certain line with her that night. And it would do. It was enough. For now.

He got to his feet and looked down at her, and Emily said lazily, 'Are you staying at your flat tonight, Giovanni?'

'No, I decided to book into a hotel this time—as I was only going to be here a couple of days.'

She got to her feet at last, not wanting him to go—and not wanting him to stay! She'd fully expected that Giovanni would suggest they spend the rest of the night together—in her bed—and she'd rehearsed in her mind the gracious way in which she would turn him down. But that obviously wasn't necessary, which was just as well, she thought. Much as she liked him—really liked him—she still thought he was probably an opportunist, someone who took his chances with no questions asked, then walked away, unscathed. Yet she had to admit that he had not behaved in any way that she'd found unattractive or unacceptable—quite the reverse! She turned resolutely to show him out, just as the phone rang stridently by her side.

It was late for a call and, raising her eyes briefly at Giovanni, she reached over to pick up the receiver. It was Coral and, after listening to several moments of excited chatter, Emily said, 'Oh, great…all right—it'll be good to have you back… What? Oh…OK, then—no, no, there's no need, we've got most things, but I'm going food shopping in the morning in any case and I'll re-stock where necessary.' Then, 'Have you enjoyed your break with the parents?' Emily shrugged, glancing over at Giovanni briefly. 'OK—see you tomorrow, Coral,' she said.

She put the phone down slowly and looked up at Giovanni, who had been watching her—watching the changing expressions on her face. 'Coral is coming home earlier than expected,' she said. 'She wasn't due back until Sunday night.' She raised her hands in mild resignation. 'But first she's going to Heathrow to pick up Nico. Apparently, he's going to be staying here with us for a week!'

# CHAPTER SIX

EARLY one morning of the following week Emily let herself quietly out of the flat so as not to disturb Nico, who was still fast asleep in Coral's room.

As she made her way swiftly towards the Underground, Emily's mobile rang. It was Giovanni, and she smiled instinctively. He'd already contacted her several times since Friday evening, not only to thank her again, but, it seemed to Emily, to just chat… About anything. About nothing. And she was honest enough to admit that, in spite of everything, she was beginning to look forward to his calls.

'*Buon giorno, signorina.*' His dark, melting tones filled Emily with the usual warm shiver of pleasure.

'Giovanni—hello…' She couldn't keep the smile from her voice. 'This is a very early call—couldn't you sleep?'

'Well, I knew the day would have started for you. And I just wanted to say hi.'

'Hi,' she said lightly.

'So—how's it going with Nico? Is he behaving himself?'

'Well, when *I'm* around he does,' Emily said. 'But, as I spent the rest of the weekend at my father's house, I haven't seen that much of him.' She shrugged. 'Anyway, I thought it was tactful to leave the two of them together.'

'That was thoughtful of you.'

'Hmm,' Emily murmured enigmatically. The fact was, she didn't want to be in Nico's company at all. As soon as Coral had arrived with him on Saturday afternoon, she was struck by the man's synthetic charm.

'I suppose Coral has to go to work this week?' Giovanni said.

'Yes, she's employed by one of the big estate agencies in town and they're very busy at the moment, so there's no prospect of her having any more time off to spend with Nico,' Emily replied. 'So, apparently he finds his way around by himself all day, meets Coral for lunch and again in the evenings. And I don't see them until quite late.' She paused. 'They seem to be enjoying themselves,' she added.

'He's lucky to have such a lovely place to stay while he's in London,' Giovanni said, 'and lucky that you were prepared to put him up.'

Emily made a face to herself. Actually, she felt quite annoyed with Coral about the whole thing. Their flat was not big enough to entertain someone who was, after all, more or less a complete stranger. But it was her friend's home as much as it was Emily's, so she kept quiet.

By this time Emily had reached the Underground. 'Well, thanks for your call, Giovanni,' she said lightly. 'I'll have to go—my train's due in.'

'Of course, Emily.' He paused. 'The weather is so wonderful today… I wish you were here so that I could drive you out into the countryside. We could have a long, long lunch at a favourite spot of mine…the food, the wine…'

'Stop!' Emily said. 'You're making my mouth water— and I haven't even had any breakfast yet! Anyway,' she added, 'aren't you expected to do any work today, like the rest of us?'

'Oh, yes—of course. I've promised to mind the shop later for Stefano, and apparently there's a sort of family meeting I have to attend this evening.' He paused. 'These are a necessary evil which take place from time to time, I'm afraid, and unfortunately Aldo will be there as well,' he added.

'Oh, yes—Aldo,' Emily said, remembering the handsome man she'd been introduced to in Rome, and wondering what it was that Giovanni didn't like about him.

Finally, they ended the call and Giovanni went into the kitchen of his flat to make his morning coffee. Glancing around at the spacious area, he couldn't help comparing it with the tiny room—not much more than a short galley—in which Emily had prepared their meal the other evening. Yet she'd handled everything with such deft efficiency, producing that fabulous meal with no apparent effort, he thought. He stopped what he was doing for a moment, remembering how he'd touched her cheek, had taken his time in removing that small trace of chocolate. He had felt such an unutterable longing to take her in his arms and cover her lips with his, to feel her feminine curves moulding to his body...and, for the briefest of seconds, he'd felt that she had wanted it, too. How had he let the opportunity pass? he asked himself—it wasn't his way to hold back. But he couldn't rid himself of the conviction that if he wanted Emily he would have to work hard to earn her respect, her love, to get her to the point where she would submit readily to his increasing physical need of her. There was a price on this woman's head, he thought, and it was nothing to do with money.

He sighed briefly as he poured boiling water onto the coffee grounds. He'd never before had to bide his time to get anywhere with a woman, was only too aware that they seemed naturally attracted to him from the start. But he couldn't be sure about Emily, feeling that he still had to get past the thin veneer that seemed to protect her from anyone—from any man—getting too close.

The damnable thing was, they were now hundreds of miles apart and prolonged absence did nothing for any relationship—Giovanni knew that well enough. A flame without oxygen would soon peter out—and there was no way that he was going to watch this particular flame die! He knew that it wouldn't be a good idea to go back to the UK straight away…Emily would definitely not appreciate being hassled or pressurized, the feeling that she was being cornered. Yet he knew he mustn't let too much time pass before seeing her again, and she could be sent anywhere abroad at any time—her firm was planning to send her to Estonia, so she'd said, but she wasn't sure when that would be. At this rate, he thought morosely, it was going to be like capturing a dainty butterfly without much of a net to do it with. He bit his lip thoughtfully, remembering seeing Emily with that man she worked with—Justin. He was a good-looking guy, a decent sort of bloke and obviously smitten with Emily—anyone could see that. Yet she clearly did not return his feelings. But why? Giovanni wondered. What, and where, was the golden key that would unlock Emily's heart?

On Thursday evening Emily arrived home earlier than usual, the boss having decided that, as everyone had been working flat out for days, he would make it a short afternoon, just keeping a skeleton staff on duty until six o'clock.

This was quite a treat, Emily thought as she unlocked her front door and ran swiftly up the stairs. She'd have a long cool shower, then maybe finish the book she was reading before thinking about her evening meal. One good thing about Nico's visit was that he and Coral always ate out, so there was no chance of her being disturbed—not for several hours.

How wrong could she be? As she went into the sitting room, Nico got up from the sofa, treating her to one of his disarming smiles.

'Oh—Nico… I didn't realize you'd be here,' Emily began awkwardly, and he interrupted.

'I hope…is OK…' he said. 'Coral is to work late tonight.' He paused. 'She suggest I come here for rest… then we go next door to Trattoria later…'

'Oh, yes…we eat at Marco's sometimes,' Emily replied, trying not to feel too disappointed that her own plans were going to be thwarted. 'The food is good—you'll enjoy it.' She paused. 'Did—did Coral say when she'd be home?'

Nico shrugged. 'She not sure…about eight o'clock— hopefully.'

Emily groaned inwardly. It was only five-thirty—how could she stand being here with Nico for nearly three hours? Why couldn't he have found something to do in town? Then she felt guilty—he was probably feeling worn out by now, having apparently trudged the streets each day to enjoy the sights, and having to suffer being jostled and pushed around by the crowds. And she had to admit that he'd not been as much of an intrusion as she'd feared, because she only really saw him later on each evening and, as soon as he and Coral came back from wherever they'd been, Emily had gone to bed almost straight away, staying up just long enough to show an interest.

'I'll make some tea—or some coffee for us in a minute,

Nico,' she said, smiling briefly at him as she went into her bedroom, shutting the door firmly.

'OK—*grazie*—' he murmured, his gaze following her as she went.

Standing for a moment with her back to the door, Emily frowned. So much for a long relaxing shower and wandering about the flat in next to nothing! she thought. Instead, she'd just have to change out of her office things, have a quick wash, then try to be an amenable hostess to their visitor. She sighed, feeling irritable all over again. To have a lovely long evening ahead, with no one but herself to please, had been such a wonderful thought... Now she was going to have to make small-talk with Coral's beau until her friend got back.

Slipping out of her clothes, she went into the bathroom next door, glancing at herself in the mirror as she soaped her face and hands. And thinking of a certain other Italian who she'd be quite happy to have lounging on her sofa. She had gone over and over the evening they'd spent together here, the way he'd gazed at her across the table with that special look in his eyes which always made her senses swim. Then she shook her head, cross at allowing herself these silly thoughts—like Nico, Giovanni was a mind-numbingly handsome Italian—a Latin charmer of women. But what about loyalty and devotion, that quality which her parents had demonstrated for the whole of their married life, and which Emily didn't dare to hope was likely to feature in her own experience. Everyone seemed different today, she thought, wanting so much more from life, and that meant new partners when the novelty wore off and boredom set in.

And what about honesty? Where a beautiful female was concerned, Emily could only believe that, for most men, the woman of the moment was all that mattered.

Presently, with her hair brushed and wearing a fitted white shirt and jeans, Emily left her bedroom and Nico, lounging on the sofa, turned lazily to look at her as she went into the kitchen.

Glancing back at him casually, she said, 'Would you like tea or coffee, Nico? Or maybe something stronger?' She smiled apologetically. 'I'm afraid that at this time of day chamomile tea is the only thing that works for me, but we've got the ordinary kind—as you know by now!'

He got to his feet and followed her into the kitchen. 'I'll have…whatever you have, Emily,' he murmured.

Emily was aware, suddenly, that she was beginning to feel uncomfortable in Nico's presence… He had come over to deliberately stand very close to her, and she had to gesture to him to move aside so that she could reach up to the shelf for the box of tea bags. Then, just as she reached upwards, she felt his arms slide around her waist, both hands resting provocatively against the flatness of her stomach, and she immediately thrust herself right away and looked up at him sharply. But he only gazed down at her, at the heightened colour of her cheeks and, narrowing his eyes briefly, he said softly, in his halting English, 'English girls are…so…enchanting…so cool…'

Then he moved back towards her again and, bending his head, he closed his lips firmly over Emily's mouth—at which unbelievable point she staggered backwards in protest.

'Nico!' she almost shouted. 'What on *earth* are you doing?'

But Nico was not going to be put off that easily and he moved towards her again, enfolding her in his arms. 'Emilee,' he said breathily, 'be nice…you are so beautiful…I cannot resist…'

Pushing him off her, she said angrily, 'Go *away*!' He raised his hands as if to say, *What's the problem? It was only a kiss*…but Emily was having none of it.

'You are totally out of order, Nico!' she said crossly. 'Do you understand what that means? It means your behaviour is not welcome! It's inappropriate! Learn those words *now,* because you're going to need them if you think you can take advantage of any woman who takes your fancy!' She swallowed, not really believing what had just happened. 'Now—go away!' she said.

He shrugged, but turned to do as she'd asked and, to her own annoyance, Emily found herself shaking inside. Nico was a tall, fit, strong young man…and practically a stranger, even if he had spent the last five nights staying in their flat. But he was Coral's guest, not hers! How dared he take that kind of liberty—because his whole attitude just now had been overwhelmingly purposeful, and she was sure that if she'd shown him the slightest encouragement things could have gone much further.

Fuming as she waited for the kettle to boil, Emily thought of her friend… Poor Coral.

As she made the tea, Emily wondered how she was going to convince Coral to let this man go out of her life before real damage was done. She could describe what had just gone on in their kitchen—but she knew she couldn't do that. It would be too hurtful. No, but somehow Coral must come around to Emily's way of thinking. Obviously, there would be many exceptions, she thought, but holiday flings spelt bad news, whatever nationality you were talking about. Here today, gone tomorrow…but what about the broken hearts left in their wake? No, Emily thought, definitely, *definitely,* not worth the risk!

\* \* \*

At the end of the following week Emily found herself once more on the plane to Rome. Her recent assignment in Italy had been so successful that the boss had decided that she should return. 'It will all become so familiar to you, Emily, you'll be like one of the locals soon,' he'd joked. 'And there's plenty of work still to do over there!'

She had received the news with a mixture of feelings… In one way it would be good to go back because she had definitely begun to feel more at home in the place, more relaxed about everything—although how much that was down to knowing Giovanni, Emily didn't like to think. But, in another, she half wished she was being sent somewhere else—anywhere else—to help her forget how much she'd begun to like Giovanni Boselli. Really like him.

His telephone calls continued with determined regularity and, although Emily's heart leapt with pleasure each time she heard his voice, she knew this was not the way she wanted it. So she decided not to tell him that she was coming to Rome for a further four days—and, in any case, he was apparently not going to be there, so there was no point.

'I'm spending a week at home in the country,' he'd said during one of his calls. 'It's very hot in town at the moment and, anyway, there's stuff to do for my mother. But soon I'll be back in England.' He'd paused. 'I want to stroll down Oxford Street with you when it's cold and frosty and when the Christmas lights are on,' he'd said, 'and we'll eat hot chestnuts together.' Why did he make it sound so good? 'I'll peel yours for you,' he'd added darkly.

Now, gazing out of the window as the plane came in to land, Emily couldn't help comparing Giovanni with Nico… Well, there was no comparison, she thought. Nico was a silly young man trying his luck with life, while

Giovanni was much more mature, more understanding… more manly, more totally acceptable. And not once had he behaved in the absurd way that Nico had, not once taken that step too far.

She'd never mentioned anything to Coral about Nico making a pass at her, keeping out of their way until it was time for him to go home, and it had been a great relief to Emily when he'd finally departed.

Now, the plane landed safely and everyone made moves to leave the aircraft. Well, Emily thought, this time it was going to be up to her. She'd have to find her own way around, eat all her meals alone… No Coral—and no Giovanni, either. So—that was good. Wasn't it?

# CHAPTER SEVEN

FOR obvious reasons, Emily chose to book herself a room at a different hotel than the one she and Coral had stayed at—she didn't want to have to make small talk with Nico, who'd be on duty again now, and who was probably already well into seduction mode again, she thought.

For the next couple of days, Emily surprised herself by finding everything so much easier. She'd learned how the public transport system worked and where to purchase tickets, and how to find short cuts through the countless winding streets until she found the places she was looking for. And, so far, there had only been one hotel which she was not going to recommend to the firm, though she hoped it wasn't only because the man on Reception reminded her of Nico!

By the fourth day of her visit, Emily had covered almost everything she had to do—which had been her deliberate plan so that she could have a few hours to herself to revisit St Peter's and the Sistine Chapel and the Raphael Rooms. To drink in all the works of art of the leading painters, though realizing that there was so much to see it would take a lifetime to absorb it all. But to be able to feast her eyes on all the glorious pictures was an amazing bonus to her job, helping to make up for her occasional minor bouts of homesickness.

It was another very hot day and, dressed in her ice-blue sundress, her sun hat pulled well down on her head and with her large dark glasses obscuring most of her face, Emily strolled along the streets towards the Basilica. There were, naturally, hundreds of people of every nationality milling around the ancient monuments—in fact, it seemed that the entire world was there—but suddenly, unbelievably and almost making her gasp out loud, she saw Giovanni's unmistakable figure. But he was supposed to be out in the country somewhere! Not here at all! He was standing outside a coffee house talking to a dark-haired, beautifully dressed woman, who was standing with her back to Emily, talking and gesticulating animatedly.

Emily stood still for a moment, not knowing what to do... Should she go up to Giovanni and announce her presence? But he'd want to know why she hadn't told him she was going to be in Rome—and she didn't have a valid answer! She could hardly tell him the truth—which was that she wanted to avoid being near him, avoid the possibility of falling in love with an Italian, it would almost certainly prove to be an unwise bet.

Quickly, Emily moved into the shelter of a nearby doorway, just as Giovanni's vivacious friend took her leave of him, walking rapidly away in the opposite direction. That had to have been the girl in the picture, Emily thought, swallowing over a dry tongue—but as the woman had turned her head her dark glasses had made it impossible to tell whether she resembled the girl in the photograph or not. But...there had been something special... intimate...about the body language between the two of them as they'd chatted. If that wasn't the girl, then it was another glamorous female in Giovanni Boselli's life. But—so what? Emily thought reasonably. He was a free individual, and how many women he had at the same time was no business of hers…just so long as *she* wasn't among their number! So what on earth was bugging her?

Emily waited until he had walked away and was out of sight before emerging from her shadowy hiding place and resuming her journey, admitting to feeling downbeat. She had not expected to see Giovanni—it was the last thing she'd thought of—and, whatever happened, she didn't want to bump into him and have to explain why she hadn't let him know she'd be in Rome again. They had had so many lengthy chats on the phone—the last one only a few hours before she'd caught her flight—it wouldn't look good that she'd omitted to mention it. And what explanation could she give?

Biting her lip until it nearly bled, Emily hurried her step a little. No, she thought, there was nothing she could say to him which wouldn't sound empty and pathetic—or insulting. So she'd better make sure that he never knew she'd been here this week.

Feeling quite overcome—and not only by the heat—she found a convenient café and lined up to buy herself a large ice cream, realizing that her problems were far from over. Soon, probably, Giovanni would be back in London. So, what then? Well, she'd meet that when the time came, she thought as, walking along, she took a generous mouthful of the minty confection. And before that, for now, she'd rest her poor senses by gazing at all those paintings.

And then, suddenly, an ear-splitting screech of brakes, quickly followed by a cacophony of screams and shouts, made Emily stop in her tracks. Just in front of her a speeding cab had half mounted the pavement, its horn still blaring, and, to her horror, she saw someone partly lying awkwardly beneath it. For a few seconds Emily stayed frozen to the spot, the shock of witnessing an accident at close hand robbing her of her power to move, and everyone around seemed to be in the same position because no one had gone forward to help. But then her lengthy course in first aid made Emily swing into action—doing nothing was not an option in these circumstances—and, yelling loudly, 'Someone—help—call an ambulance—quickly!' she dropped her ice cream and broke into a run, pushing her way past the groups of horrified spectators and dropping down onto her knees beside the prostrate victim. It was a young woman who—to Emily's relief—was sobbing and crying hysterically, which meant that her airways weren't blocked and that she could breathe unaided. She was trying desperately to raise herself up but, as she was trapped beneath the cab—fortunately clear of the wheels—there wasn't the space to do so. And by now an evil-looking gash was visible along her forehead and there was a lot of blood coursing down her arm, staining the road beneath her as her terrified eyes looked up beseechingly at Emily.

*'Aiuto! Aiuto! Per favore!'* she cried.

Emily forced herself to smile reassuringly as she grasped both the woman's hands in hers. 'It's OK…you're OK…stay still…you're going to be fine,' she said firmly, cursing the fact that she spoke so little Italian. But words of comfort in any language were easy enough to understand, she thought. 'What is your name… Name? Name?' she repeated. 'What is your name?'

'Anna,' the woman answered at once, trying to raise her head, and Emily's smile of relief broadened.

'Hello, Anna—I'm Emily,' she said, pointing to herself.

'Em—i—lee… Someone will come soon to help us.' She squeezed the trembling hands tighter. 'Try and keep still,' she said gently, 'in case you've hurt your back or your neck.' Her controlled tones seemed to quieten the sobbing, which was becoming quieter as they stayed locked together on the dusty road. Seeing that most of the blood seemed to be coming from a large wound on the girl's upper arm, Emily frantically unzipped her bag and took out the handful of tissues she'd brought with her, folding them quickly into a firm pad, which she pressed against the damaged area.

'Here—press this tightly, Anna…press…press…' Anna understood, doing as she was told.

Anna had not taken her eyes from Emily's consoling features and, with an instinctive movement, Emily put out her hand to move a stray lock of hair, sticky with blood, from the woman's forehead. 'You're doing so well, Anna,' she said. 'How old are you? How old are you…how old?'

After a moment, the girl got the message and she whimpered, 'Twenty years.'

'You are very pretty, Anna,' Emily said, smiling. 'Don't worry—they will soon get you cleaned up and back home…'

And then at last someone else did arrive, and stooped down beside them. And, with an overwhelming gush of thankfulness, Emily saw that Giovanni was right there, close to her. She looked up at him quickly, all other thoughts now far from her mind at that moment. 'This is Anna,' she said briefly, 'and it's only just happened. I don't know how badly she's hurt, but she's breathing OK, and talking…'

Hardly glancing at Emily, Giovanni took control immediately and, with both hands on the girl's shoulders, he spoke to her, asking questions in rapid Italian, his voice gentle but authoritative. Anna answered him equally quickly, responding to his persuasive sympathy, by this time her sole attention on the handsome face of the man crouching down beside her.

A few moments after that, with sirens blaring, the ambulance and *polizia* arrived on the scene and at last Emily stood back to allow the professionals to do their work. Giovanni was speaking to them, explaining as much as he knew about the accident, before coming over to Emily and taking her arm firmly, his face expressionless. At his touch she felt like bursting into tears. It's no good, she thought, nobody told you how frightened you'd feel if you had to help at a real accident, or a real heart attack…because now she was trembling all over, and even her teeth were starting to chatter.

Looking down at her seriously, Giovanni started leading her away from the scene and, feeling the comforting strength of his body, Emily found that she was able to walk calmly along beside him.

Neither spoke for a few minutes as Giovanni allowed her to recover from the recent ordeal, but as each second passed Emily knew that she had some explaining to do.

'Well, that was the last thing I expected to come across,' she said shakily, looking up at him.

'And you were the last person I expected to see,' he replied, not looking back at her, but with a pleasant enough smile on his lips.

Emily swallowed. 'Yes, I'm sorry I didn't let you know I was coming to Italy this week… It was…difficult…' she stuttered. How utterly vapid did *that* sound?

'Never mind,' he said. 'First things first. We'd better get you cleaned up.'

Cleaned up? Suddenly realization set in as Emily stared

down and with a quick intake of breath she saw the damage she'd sustained. She hadn't given herself a thought! Her pale outfit was covered in blood and gravel—probably beyond repair. What a total mess she looked!

Now he did look down at her, properly, before guiding her around the corner and into a quiet bar. 'I think you need a brandy,' he said briefly. 'Then we'll go to my flat and see what can be done. For both of us,' he added, because his own cream trousers were stained and dirty, Emily saw now.

At this time of the early afternoon there were few people in the cool and darkened bar and, removing her sunglasses, Emily sank gratefully onto the chair which Giovanni held out for her, noting impassively that in the panic she'd managed to lose her sun hat.

After ordering their drinks from the waiter, he sat alongside her, leaning back in the chair and gazing at her quizzically. But he didn't ask any questions, only thinking how ravishingly lovely Emily looked, even in her present state. The fact that her clothes were crumpled and stained did not seem to detract from her in any way. In fact, vulnerability could be a seductive state, he thought. Her hair was tousled, there was dried blood on her hands and arms and dirt on her flushed cheeks, and every now and again he saw her shiver, as if the effect of the traumatic event she had just been part of refused to leave her alone. At that moment he wanted to crush her in his arms, to hold her close to him, to make her feel safe. But he knew that would not be a wise move—especially as it was obvious that she'd not wanted him to know she'd be in Rome. He frowned briefly, looking away and trying to harden his heart against her. What had he done to make her so…elusive? To him, she seemed a complete mystery.

Their two double brandies arrived and, picking hers up, Emily sipped at the warming liquid, looking at Giovanni over the rim of her glass. 'This is good,' she murmured, drinking again more freely, and he cautioned her.

'Take it easy, Emily. Don't rush it. You've had a shock and it'll take a little time for you to recover.' He smiled at her disarmingly, now. 'If you drink it down in one, I'll be obliged to carry you back home!'

He knew what he was talking about, and Emily put her glass down, relieved to note that by now her hands had actually stopped shaking. Smiling back at him, she felt the alcohol taking effect and almost at once she began to relax.

'So—how's the job going this time?' he enquired casually. 'Finding your way around OK…? No problems?'

Emily took a deep breath. He was purposely being kind, she thought, not quizzing her about her unexpected presence in the city and assuming that for her it was business as usual. So she would treat it in the same way.

'I've done brilliantly, thanks,' she said, picking up her glass again. 'And I've finished it all in record time, so there's a chance for me to do some touristy stuff before I go back home tomorrow…I want to see some more paintings.'

'Of course you do,' he said blandly, not taking his eyes from her face and noting that her colour was deepening by the second.

Emily could stand it no longer—she *had* to say something! 'Look, I'm sorry I didn't let you know I'd be here,' she said, trying to keep her voice normal. 'But…I…I was afraid of being a nuisance to you…I thought you'd feel obliged to…you know…offer your help, waste your valuable time on me…' *How* had she managed to think that one up? 'And, also, I felt I should really attempt to get things right by myself,' she went on. 'I have a tendency to rely on other people sometimes…to let them do some of the work for me.' That was a lie, too. 'And you said that you had important work to do for your mother this week… I just didn't want to get in the way, that's all.'

Emily hoped that this explanation sounded more truthful to him than it did to her—but she was grateful for the little lies which had conveniently formed on her tongue.

Giovanni smiled at her slowly, as if considering what she had just said. 'You could never get in my way, Emily,' he murmured. 'You should know that by now. But thank you for your consideration,' he added.

That made Emily feel even worse. 'Besides, you said you wouldn't be in Rome, in any case…that you'd be in the country,' she said quickly.

'That is true,' he said coolly, 'but something came up and I had to drop back here briefly. But I'll be returning to the country later on this afternoon.'

Emily decided that she wanted to change the subject as quickly as possible. 'That accident,' she said, picking up her glass, 'it all happened in a split second. I was standing about fifty metres away, I suppose, and the first thing I saw was the cab mounting the pavement. But the noise! It was incredible! And people were screaming but no one seemed to be doing anything and when I got there that poor girl was frantic, and she couldn't get up and I was afraid to try and move her in case she'd really hurt her back, and then all that blood! It was horrible!' Emily shivered again. 'I think I remembered everything I'd been taught, but when the moment arrives and something is actually happening it's much, much worse than you ever thought it could be!' She paused for a moment to take another drink. 'I was so…so pleased when you turned up, Giovanni,' she said truthfully. 'At that moment, you seemed like a ministering angel!'

'I think the ministering angel was already there,' he said gently.

Giovanni had let her relive the experience, knowing that she had to get it out of her system, and he shrugged at her words. 'I heard all the commotion,' he said. 'That's what alerted me that something was going on. And, when I got there, all I saw was someone—who turned out to be you—kneeling on the pavement and talking to someone underneath the cab… It didn't take me too long to put two and two together,' he added drily. He paused. 'But I'm gratified to think that you were…pleased…to see me, Emily.'

Emily looked away quickly. From the way he'd just said that, he'd made it clear that he was feeling slightly hurt about her secretive behaviour—and also that he probably didn't believe her explanation about it. She sighed, wishing now that she had told him she'd be here again… Things would have been a whole lot easier for her!

For a while they sat in silence while Emily sipped and sipped at the brandy. Giovanni had got it exactly right, knowing it was what she'd need to calm her. She couldn't care less about her appearance, which seemed totally irrelevant now, the curious looks from one or two other drinkers passing her by unnoticed. She felt comfortable, relaxed—and sublimely at ease.

But not for long.

'Why didn't you tell me you'd be here, Emily?' he asked softly. 'What was the real reason? Tell me the truth.'

She waited a moment before answering. Then, 'I…I don't want to find myself in a position I might…regret…' she began, and he frowned.

'How so?' he asked.

'I'm afraid to get involved in something—or with someone—that might turn out badly,' she said, wishing that the words would come more easily.

'Why—don't you trust me?' he asked, and his tone was sombre.

'I don't think I trust myself—or fate—' she said slowly. 'And I'm unsure of...of...'

'Of Italians?' He finished the sentence for her. 'Have you known many, Emily?'

'Not many,' she admitted, 'and certainly not in a close, personal sense. But there *is* a cultural difference between us. Well, I think so anyway.' She paused. 'Your young men can be...impulsive sometimes and...and...' She wanted to say *audacious* but that would be going too far. Giovanni had never been audacious with her. It was the wretched Nico who was in the forefront of her mind as she spoke.

His expression had darkened as she'd been speaking, and he caught and held her gaze. 'I think you should explain that,' he said coolly.

'OK, I will,' Emily said, equally coolly. 'You remember me telling you about Nico—Coral's friend—the guy who stayed at our flat recently?'

'Of course.'

'Well, one evening I got home early from work—Coral wouldn't be back until later—and Nico was there, resting for a couple of hours.' She paused, feeling angry again at the way the man had behaved. 'So I offered to make him some tea, and when I was in the kitchen he came in and...and...'

'Go on,' Giovanni said, frowning.

'Well, let's just say that he took advantage of me,' Emily said. 'And I told him that he was out of order. That his attentions were unwelcome.' She grimaced. 'He seems to think that he's God's gift to womankind and, worse, it didn't occur to him that he was betraying Coral—who, after all, was putting herself out to see that he had a good time in London.'

'What did he actually do?' Giovanni persisted.

'He put his arms around me and kissed me, full on the mouth. And invited me to "be nice"—which, to my mind, meant only one thing,' Emily said flatly.

'But it didn't get any worse than that?' Giovanni asked.

'How much worse should it have got?' Emily said, suddenly irritated at his reaction—which shouldn't have surprised her, she thought. It confirmed her opinion that Italian men were passionate, intense—and ready to seize the moment.

'But…there was no attempt to take it further?' Giovanni went on. He paused. 'I think I can safely say that, as a general rule, we are lovers of beautiful women.'

'Oh, really? Well, that's a comforting thought!' Emily said crossly. He wasn't taking any of this seriously, she thought, clearly giving the subject little significance. But it was significant to her.

'I do believe that you are "lovers of women",' she said after a moment. 'But what I don't believe is that one woman—speaking generally, of course—would ever be enough…that you're not really into long-term relationships—the sort which require loyalty, fidelity…and total commitment,' she added, her eyes filling suddenly.

'Oh, and you think that fecklessness is confined to our race?' Giovanni asked scornfully. 'Have a good look at your own social statistics, Emily. British marriages, relationships, have a very bad track record. If you're making odious comparisons, you'd better be careful in your assumptions.'

Emily realized that she *was* making assumptions—and her sense of justice made her hesitate. 'Yes, well, I'm sorry if I'm jumping to conclusions,' she said slowly, not wanting to admit that this was her own problem more than anything else. The dark-eyed, amorous Italians whom she had met did seem to have that special way with them which, at times, could be almost irresistible, their passionate instincts often equally matched by a caring, cherishing attitude which could melt the heart. They had the ability to make a woman feel she was a desired female who they wanted to love, admire and protect... Yet all the time she felt a nagging doubt that they could sustain that initial glow, that it was instinctive for the hot-blooded Italian to search out as many females as he needed to satisfy his carnal ambitions. And she was determined not to allow herself to become trapped by their powerful allure—a characteristic exhibited so captivatingly by the man at her side.

No more was said for a while as they finished their drinks and presently, aware that Emily had regained total self-control, Giovanni stood up. 'Come on. Let's get you to the flat and a wash in some warm water.' He glanced down at her. 'It's rather far to walk from here so we'll get a cab.'

'Maybe I should go straight back to the hotel,' Emily suggested, and he shrugged.

'Whatever you like,' he said, 'but I think it would be preferable for you to clean up and relax at my place first.'

Emily stood up then, too, surprised at how strange her legs felt. 'Yes, OK, we'll do that,' she agreed, thinking that, at the moment, if he suggested a trip to outer space she'd agree.

He took her arm as they left the bar. 'Besides,' he said, 'there's someone there I'd like you to meet.'

'Oh?' Emily looked up at him, surprised. Then realization struck. The woman he'd been talking to had to be the woman in the picture! Emily hadn't been close enough to have a good look, but it was obvious now, she thought. She was going to be introduced to that beautiful face—and Giovanni Boselli seemed to have no difficulty in bringing another woman into the equation.

Well, there was nothing for it, she'd have to fall in with his plans now, she thought, as they sat together in the cab, which sped at breakneck speed through the teeming streets. When they eventually arrived at the flat it seemed even more auspicious than it had before, as they entered the coolness of the large hallway.

'Ah, good, she's back already,' Giovanni said casually, seeing that his front door was wide open. 'She said she wouldn't be long,' he added, 'because we're leaving the city in an hour.'

As they went inside, a woman, hearing them come in, called from the kitchen, 'Coffee!'

Giovanni grinned down at Emily. 'Good, just what you need,' he said.

Just then the woman entered the sitting room carrying a tray and, with a jolt of surprise, Emily looked across at the attractive dark-eyed face…but it was not the face in the photograph, she realized as a thousand thoughts formed in her mind at the same time.

Giovanni gazed down at Emily. 'I'd like you to meet my mother, Emilee-a,' he said softly, pronouncing her name in that special way of his, making Emily's tongue go dry with desire. And to the woman he said, 'And this is Emily, Mamma—you remember me telling you about her?'

# CHAPTER EIGHT

EMILY hoped that the look of total surprise wasn't written all over her face. This was certainly the same woman she'd seen talking to Giovanni earlier—but it was his mother, not his girlfriend! She was good-looking, short and about sixty years old, Emily guessed, and she had obviously looked after herself, her overall appearance still extremely attractive. She was dressed in a sheer cream skirt and smart summer shoes, her loose lemon top setting off her black hair and dark complexion. And her large, bright gold hoop earrings glistened in the afternoon sunlight, adding to the glamorous picture she presented to the world. She had Giovanni's searching eyes—which were raised questioningly now, as she stared at Emily, then at her son, then back at Emily.

'What on *earth* has got you both into this state?' she demanded, her English heavily accented. She turned to her son. 'Giovanni?'

Giovanni took a few moments to explain briefly what had happened earlier, and his mother put down the tray she'd been holding and came over to Emily, her hand outstretched.

'*Mamma Mia!*… How terrible! How terrible!' she exclaimed, then she broke into a smile. 'I am Maria,' she said, her voice warm, 'and I am pleased to meet you…to meet another of my son's many friends.'

Emily smiled back in response, taking Maria's hand lightly. 'Thank you, Maria.' She looked down at herself, then back at the woman. 'I am sorry to be in such a mess,' she said. 'Maybe I can do something about it in a minute, before I go back to my hotel?'

Giovanni picked up the tray with the two mugs on it. 'Sit down and have a coffee first, Emily,' he said. 'I'll go and make another one for myself,' he added, as he handed his mother hers.

Emily did as she was told, sitting down carefully on the pale chaise longue by the window—where she'd lain down once before, she remembered wryly. The room seemed vast in the daylight, she thought, glancing around her briefly, its tiled floor cool beneath her feet. And still there in the centre of the cabinet in front of her was that picture. Still smiling, those bewitching eyes sending out their message to any onlooker. *This is my place; this is where I belong,* it seemed to say.

Maria sat down then, a little way from Emily, but looking at her with a rather inscrutable expression on her face. Neither spoke for a moment as they sipped their coffee.

Then, 'I can't tell you how thankful I was when Giovanni suddenly showed up,' Emily said earnestly. 'I was the only person who seemed to be offering any assistance—and goodness knows, I could do very little. The way the poor girl was trapped made it impossible for me to find out if she was seriously injured, or even to put her into the recovery position.'

'You have medical experience?' Maria asked.

'No, but after my mother died I attended several first aid courses,' she said. 'I wanted to have at least some understanding of what to do in an emergency.' She didn't add that it had been her father who was uppermost in her mind. What if he suffered something dramatic, as her mother had done, and she, Emily, was there and not able to help? She shuddered. 'I'll be having nightmares about that accident for a few weeks, I expect. I felt so utterly helpless,' she added.

'But, from what Giovanni said, you were not helpless. You did the only thing which was possible at the time,' Maria said firmly. 'You were the one who gave her courage and reassurance.'

Emily took another sip of coffee. 'Well, I felt a whole lot better when Giovanni took over,' she said, 'and it's a good thing he was here in Rome.' Not bothering to add that she'd thought he was miles away in the country somewhere.

'Yes, well, if this had all happened tomorrow, instead of today, he would not have been in the city,' Maria said. 'He is taking me back home later… I travelled in to do some shopping today,' she added, smiling.

Just then, Giovanni returned with his coffee and sat down opposite them, and after a few moments Maria said, 'Giovanni tells me you are in the travel business, Emily.'

'Yes. That's right.'

'Do you enjoy that?'

Emily hesitated. 'Sometimes I do,' she said. 'But in every job there are highs and lows. I am not always thrilled to be away from home quite so much,' she admitted.

'So—what would you like to be doing—ideally?' Maria asked, and Emily began to feel that she was being interviewed!

Giovanni spoke for her. 'What she would really like to be doing is painting her pictures, full time, Mamma,' he said. 'Emily is an amazing painter—in my opinion, professional.'

Maria's eyes had narrowed slightly during this conversation, and she was staring at Emily closely—and the girl was very conscious of the fact. Well, everyone knew what Italian mothers were like where their precious sons were concerned, Emily thought. No woman was ever good enough for them, and Maria probably feared that Emily had designs on Giovanni. She finished her drink and put her mug down on the little table beside her. Maria need have no worries on *that* score, she thought.

Presently, Maria stood up, taking control. 'Go into the bathroom, Emily, and have a warm wash,' she instructed firmly. 'Then we will see about your clothes.' She put her head on one side. 'I think we can sponge the dirt off—but all that blood will need a cold water soak, I'm afraid,' she added.

Emily turned obediently to do as she was told and Giovanni stood as well, barring her way slightly. 'No, I think my en suite will be more suitable, Mamma.' He pointed to a door along the hallway. 'There's the bedroom—with facilities,' he said. 'Make yourself at home, Emily.'

Feeling as if she were in a strange kind of dream, Emily did as she was told. What was going on? She was supposed to be somewhere else, relaxing and admiring all those fabulous ancient paintings this afternoon, not here in Giovanni's flat—with his mother in attendance. And not with her clothes in this state, either. She'd only worn this designer dress once before; she made a face to herself. Was it any good, ever, to make plans? she thought. Life had a will of its own—well, hers certainly seemed to have at the moment and you just had to go with the flow. Go where it took you.

Giovanni's bedroom was spacious and cool, the king-size bed neatly made, its white covers smooth and inviting—and for a heady moment, Emily felt like stretching out on it for a short nap! Instead, she pushed open the other door in the room, revealing the en suite bathroom, and gazed at it in admiration. There was a massive corner bath with shower, the glistening porcelain and gold taps almost blinding her as she looked around, and there were fluffy white towels in abundance everywhere. The place was to die for, and if all this belonged to her, Emily thought, this was where she'd be spending a lot of her time! She paused for a moment…Giovanni undoubtedly had good taste— not to mention very expensive taste.

As she went inside, closing the door behind her, she suddenly noticed a long pink gossamer-like negligee hanging on a hook, and she caught her breath. That certainly did not belong to Giovanni! It was exquisite, and she let the fine folds slip between her fingers as she touched it gently. It was a young woman's—obviously *that* young woman's, who must have been staying here with Giovanni… So, *that* was what had brought him back… 'briefly'…he'd said!

Going over to the basin, she glanced up at the shelf above, her eye immediately caught by the sight of an exotic flask of the most fashionable scent from one of France's renowned perfumeries. And it was not for the Giovannis of this world!

Emily sat on the edge of the bath for a moment. Why did all this matter to her? None of it was any of her business! And Giovanni Boselli was nothing to her— nothing at all! Who he chose to entertain at his flat was of no interest to her whatsoever! Then another thought struck her… Of course! This had to be Maria's! That was it! Giovanni had mentioned once that his mother sometimes stayed at the flat.

Presently, she rejoined the others and Maria looked appraisingly at Emily's appearance. Somehow the girl had managed to make herself quite presentable again, had been able to sponge off most of the dirt from her dress.

'That's better,' Maria said gently, 'though there is still some work to be done on those blood stains.'

Emily smiled. 'My dry-cleaners have worked miracles in the past,' she said. 'I'll be leaving this up to them.'

'I'll take you back to your hotel now, Emily—if that's what you would like,' Giovanni said, looking down at her, and she smiled quickly.

'Thank you, yes, I don't think I'll be doing any sight-seeing today after all,' she said, thinking that an early night suddenly seemed very attractive. As Giovanni left the room for a moment, she turned to Maria, holding out her hand. 'It's been great to have met you, Maria,' she said. She paused. 'And I hope you don't mind me mentioning it, but…the negligee hanging behind the door just now…is absolutely beautiful. I don't think I've ever seen anything quite so lovely.'

Maria frowned, then shrugged slightly. 'Lingerie? Oh, no, I have not left any lingerie here,' she said. 'In fact, I haven't stayed here for months.' She shook her head. 'No, no—Rome is far too hot for me at this time of year.'

As Giovanni drove them out of the city later, Maria glanced briefly across at her son, her heart swelling with pride, as usual. He was so like his father, she thought for the hundredth time…not only handsome, but kind, thoughtful and diligent. He had accepted his respon-sibilities so young, and with not a single grumble, had been *too* hardworking, of course, handling that dreadful company matter—which Maria did not want to think about—with such adroitness, such natural skill. Her mouth tightened slightly. It had been good to see him with the Englishwoman today… Maria had begun to despair of him ever showing that kind of interest in a female again. And she had to admit that there was something about Emily that was particularly endearing—even to her. She gazed out of the window for a moment and cleared her throat.

'I think I can understand why you like this…Emily…' she began tentatively, trying to find the right words. Well, he would be expecting her to pass *some* opinion, but the past had taught Maria to be cautious. She would never make the same mistake again.

'It would be hard for anyone not to like Emily,' he replied casually, not taking his eyes from the road. His lip curled slightly. 'The sad fact is that it's harder to get her to like me. That's the problem.'

Maria was aghast! 'Why? What are you saying… What is it?' she demanded.

'I wish I knew,' Giovanni replied soberly. Then, after a second, he added, 'She is…warm, yes, but…not close. It is so strange.' He hesitated. 'I have no experience with that kind of woman.'

Maria would have none of it. 'She *does* like you, Giovanni, there is no doubt about that! I could tell straight away! I assure you that…'

'Yes, I think she does, Mamma,' he interrupted, 'but not in the way that I would…wish.'

Then neither of them spoke for a few moments after that, Giovanni admitting to still feeling shattered that Emily hadn't told him she was going to be in Rome, while Maria was quietly seething inside. How any woman could hold her son at arm's length was beyond belief—and she knew what he was getting at all right! She was Italian too,

was she not, with the same passionate blood in her veins…
had been loved by her husband in the way that only Italians
could love! Still, she decided to say no more. She had said
too much before—and look what had happened.

Presently, she said, 'Will you be seeing her again soon,
*carissimo*?'

Giovanni shrugged. 'I don't know… Of course, I can
find excuses to visit the London office, and I will try to
see her then, but my duties recommence here again soon
and I must say that I'm looking forward to it, Mamma. The
idea of six months off was pleasant, but…'

'Was necessary,' Maria said firmly.

'OK. But I want to get back in harness now, as soon as
possible. You've been holding the fort for too long.'

Maria smiled. 'With help from others, of course,' she
said. 'And our profits are holding up well, *carissimo*. Have
no fear about that.'

Emily had booked an early flight for the following morning,
and it was with some relief that she boarded the aircraft.
Yesterday had been a day to remember, she thought—and
not for particularly good reasons. Coming across that
accident had sobered her more than she cared to admit, and
meeting Maria Boselli in Giovanni's flat had been a totally
unexpected incident. Maria had been kind enough—in a sort
of way, Emily thought—but there was something going on
behind those shrewd, dark eyes that had made the girl feel
slightly uncomfortable. She shrugged inwardly. Maria was
the archetypal possessive Italian mother. Emily had heard the
two of them speaking in low tones while she'd been tidying
herself up—and she couldn't help feeling that she was being
discussed… She'd heard Giovanni's voice raised slightly
now and again, as if they were arguing about something.

Now, staring out of the window as the aeroplane left the ground, Emily remembered the last thing which had been said, as they'd made their goodbyes yesterday, and she smiled faintly to herself.

'Next time you're in Italy, you must visit us, Emily,' Maria had said in a tone which implied a directive rather than an invitation. 'La Campagna is the place to be at this time of the year…Giovanni will bring you.'

And Emily had accepted the suggestion graciously, while thinking there was more chance of being flown to the moon than of her visiting the Boselli family home. She was not going to get involved any more with Giovanni… Deep down, all her instincts told her to get out now, while there was still time.

Emily decided to prepare a special supper for herself and Coral on Friday evening. They'd not seen much of each other recently—with Nico being there, and then with Emily having to go away again so soon. It would be good to have a catch-up, she thought now.

Coral arrived home earlier than usual and, when she heard their front door close, Emily called from the kitchen, 'Hi, Coral…dinner's in forty minutes—you've time for a shower.'

Coral came and stood by the door, leaning against it for a moment as she watched Emily prepare the sea bass. Emily looked across, smiling.

'It's good to be home,' she commented, reaching for the black pepper. 'I hope they don't send me anywhere for a week or two—anyway, I've had enough of Rome for the moment,' she added.

'I'm sure you have, and you must tell me all about it,' Coral said, and there was something in her voice that made Emily look up quickly. 'I will have that shower,' Coral went on, 'but first, I could do with a drink.' She yawned. 'Do you want one? I'll open one of the bottles of red we brought back with us from Italy.'

'OK, fine,' Emily said as she started slicing some tomatoes for the salad. 'You sound tired, Coral—hectic at work?'

'No, actually, it's dead quiet at the moment and we're all bored out of our minds.' She paused. 'A flat day can seem twice as long as usual—but you wouldn't know anything about that.'

Presently, after they'd finished their supper—which Coral was very complimentary about—the two girls sat, elbows on the table in the window, drinking their coffee. Emily glanced at Coral briefly. She didn't really want to mention Nico's name at all, but it seemed odd not to say *something* about him—after all, he had occupied their flat for a week.

'Has Nico been in touch?' she asked casually. 'I hope he enjoyed himself as much as he thought he would—you certainly showed him all the sights while he was here.'

'Oh, yes, he's phoned a couple of times,' Coral said casually.

'And…um…have you made plans for him to come back at some point?' Emily went on, thinking that Coral wasn't being particularly talkative—she'd have expected her sometimes excitable friend to reveal all the details without this sort of prompting.

'No…well, we'll have to see,' Coral said. She drank some coffee. 'It was just one of those things…you know, with Nico…he's a nice enough bloke but…Italians are different, aren't they…I mean, they seem so…I would never be sure…' Her voice trailed off. So, Emily thought, it had taken a week of being full-on with Nico to make Coral have second thoughts. Poor Coral—any hopes she might have had for a whirlwind affair—and possibly even something more—with a seductive Italian had somehow turned out to be disappointingly not the case. And it was clearly the reason for the girl's rather melancholy spirit this evening. Involuntarily, Emily reached over and squeezed Coral's hand for a second.

'I totally agree with you about the Latin male,' she said. 'They're a race apart in the emotional stakes and I, personally, would think more than twice about getting involved with one of them.'

Coral raised her eyes briefly. 'What—not even with the gorgeous Giovanni?' she said. 'He certainly only had eyes for you when we were in Rome, and you've said he's been on the phone since…'

Emily bit her lip, looking away quickly. 'No, not even with him, Coral,' she said.

'Did you see him this week while you were over there?'

Emily hesitated. She'd intended not to say a word about any of it, but so much had happened that she couldn't be that evasive—not with Coral. They usually confided in each other.

'Well, now you mention it, I did see him,' she said. 'He didn't even know I was going to be in Italy because I decided not to tell him, but then, out of the blue…suddenly there he was.' She went on to describe everything about the accident and going back to Giovanni's flat and meeting his mother.

'And I think my summer dress is probably ruined,' she added. 'Even if I manage to remove all the stains, I'll never feel the same about it again.'

She paused for a second, deciding not to mention the woman in the photograph, or the negligee she'd seen in Giovanni's en suite bathroom. There was no need to go into all that because it didn't matter now. It was irrelevant.

Coral blew through her teeth, suitably impressed at what Emily had just told her. That's unbelievable, Ellie,' she said. 'It's as if you're a magnet to the man. He seems to know exactly where to find you.'

'Well, somehow I've got to persuade him that I don't appreciate his company,' Emily said flatly. 'It's not as if he's ever likely to be short of female company. I won't exactly be depriving him, will I?'

'Hardly,' Coral said. 'He has to be the most mind-numbingly handsome man on the planet.' She shot a brief glance at Emily. 'He even beats Nico in that department.'

'Oh, they're all the same,' Emily said a trifle scathingly. 'So good-looking it's abnormal. And they think all women are ready to fall at their feet.'

'Well, then, here are two who are definitely *not!*' Coral said, her cheeks flushed from too much wine. She raised her glass. 'Here's to us, Ellie—and the blessed joys of a single life!'

Emily got up to make some more coffee just as her mobile rang. She glanced back at Coral. 'Phone's there behind you on the windowsill, Coral,' she said. 'Answer it, will you?'

Coral did as she was asked and in a second she stood up, following Emily into the kitchen, her eyes bright. 'It's *him—Giovanni,*' she whispered. 'Shall I say you're not here?'

Reluctantly, Emily shook her head briefly, taking the phone from Coral. 'Hi…Gio…' she began, then her expression changed as she listened for a few moments.

'OK—yes, of course…no, I'll be here all weekend… Of course I will, Giovanni.'

She snapped the phone shut and looked across at Coral, who was staring at her open-mouthed. 'You're *going* to see him—after all we've just been *saying,*' Coral accused.

'The man has got you in his clutches, Ellie, and there's nothing you can do about it.'

'You wait and see,' Emily said shortly. 'But, for the moment, what I can do is offer him some support.'

'Why—what's going on?' Coral demanded.

'He's going to be in London mid-morning tomorrow— his best friend was taken dangerously ill yesterday, and is in hospital on a life-support machine.' She paused. 'Giovanni's asked me to meet him…to go with him to the hospital, and I couldn't refuse, could I? He sounded terrible!' She shrugged helplessly. Giovanni had seemed so upset, so unlike his normal confident self, it had almost unnerved her. It was obvious that he needed her—needed her badly—and she'd be there for him, of course she would. She'd do the same for anyone.

# CHAPTER NINE

LATE the following afternoon they left the hospital, and Giovanni held Emily's hand tightly as they waited to cross the busy road. Glancing up at him briefly, she could see how shocked he still was.

'How long did you say you've known Rupert?' she asked matter-of-factly, thinking that Giovanni wouldn't want to talk about anything else at the moment. 'You said you met up at university…?'

'Before that,' he said shortly. 'We were at boarding school together—aged thirteen. So we go back more than twenty years.' He shook his head briefly. 'It was terrible to see him lying there like that, Emily… His parents are absolutely distraught. They haven't left his side, of course.' He looked down at her. 'I felt very touched—honoured, in a way—that I'm the only one, apparently, apart from his parents, who's allowed to see him. For now, of course,' he added hurriedly. 'As soon as he's better, he'll obviously be allowed lots of visitors.'

Emily didn't look at Giovanni as he spoke. They both knew that he was being deliberately optimistic that his friend might recover—from the little she knew, it was probably less than a fifty-fifty chance. And she had been more than happy to keep out of the way downstairs in the restaurant while Giovanni had been at Rupert's bedside.

'Well, you are obviously someone very special,' she began lightly.

He cut in, 'I think I've probably known him the longest, out of our crowd,' he said. 'Wherever we've been over the years, we've always kept in touch…I've stayed with him and his family in England many times, and he pops over to our place in Italy whenever he feels like it. My mother is very fond of him,' he added.

'Have the doctors been forthcoming about Rupert's condition…? Have they offered any prognosis?' Emily asked as they walked slowly along in the late afternoon sunshine, and he shook his head briefly.

'For a man of his age to collapse so suddenly like that—so dramatically—is not, apparently, unknown,' Giovanni said. 'One good thing—his heart is still strong—so it's to do with his brain, I believe…' Giovanni stopped for a moment, unable to go on. Then, 'He hasn't regained consciousness yet.' He paused, moving to one side of the pavement to let a woman and two young children go past them, before taking Emily's hand again. 'They're not sure how deep the coma is yet.' He bit his lip. 'It must be hell for his parents—Rupert's their only child. I tried to say the right things, you know, to offer a crumb of comfort—but what do *I* know?'

Emily squeezed his hand tightly, looking up at him. 'Whatever you said, Giovanni, I'm sure it was just the right thing,' she murmured.

'Well, it was little enough, goodness only knows,' he said. 'But they did seem pleased to see me—his mother hugged me so hard I didn't think she was ever going to let me go.'

'Then that says it all,' Emily said quickly. 'Just being there with them was enough.' She hesitated. 'What happens now? Must you go straight back to Italy?'

'No—the stuff I was going to do at home can wait. I told Rupert's parents I'll be staying in England until his condition stabilizes, and the situation is clearer.'

Giovanni looked down at her suddenly, loving the feel of her fingers entwined in his, gaining strength from her closeness. Why had Emily been the first—the only—one he'd thought to ring with the bad news? He could have got in touch with any of his and Rupert's friends, but it hadn't occurred to him to do that. There was something about Emily that seemed to warm him right through… He'd felt it from the moment he'd sold her that marmalade jar in Stefano's shop, had seen how she'd reacted to the accident in Rome. Of course, she was an intensely desirable woman by anyone's standards, but it went beyond that. He tried to pin down his thoughts about her, but couldn't, and he breathed in deeply. At this moment he felt like sweeping her off her feet and carrying her into the park they were approaching and making love to her under the trees in broad daylight. Glancing down at her, he was deeply ashamed of his lustful thoughts—especially today of all days—but he was aware that times of shock, or fear, or sudden turbulence could unhinge the male psyche… The last twenty-four hours certainly seemed to have unhinged *him,* he thought.

It was typical of Emily not to prattle on with unnecessary conversation, or to recite platitudes about Rupert's present condition… She seemed perfectly content to stroll along without saying anything, or expecting him to fill the silence. He wished he had the courage to put his arm around her and draw her into him… but something told him not to do that. He frowned briefly. When she'd been in Rome and they'd been unexpectedly thrown together again during that accident, he'd felt a distinct change in their relationship which might have given him some hope for the future. For a short time she had clung to him emotionally—and he'd revelled in her obvious need for him. But then, back at the flat a distinct change seemed to have taken place in her attitude. He shrugged inwardly. He didn't understand this woman—and he doubted that he'd ever be given the time or opportunity to find out what made her tick.

Bringing him abruptly out of his introspection, Emily suddenly said, 'Where will you be staying while you're here?'

'Oh, I've booked in at my usual hotel,' he said non-committally.

Feeling slightly awkward that he might feel he had to take her out somewhere this evening, Emily said, 'I don't imagine you've made any plans for tonight, Giovanni, but you're welcome to come back home to our place for a meal. Only if you want to,' she added hurriedly. 'Coral will be delighted to see you again.'

Giovanni hesitated. 'Well, if you're absolutely sure I won't be in the way, Emily,' he said, 'it would be good to relax somewhere more like home this evening.'

'Great,' Emily said. 'It's Coral's turn to do the food tonight, and she's a good cook. I think lamb cutlets are on the menu.' She glanced up at him quickly—the expression on his handsome features was unusually hard, the normally seductive eyes seemed to have become distant and solemn—not surprisingly, she thought. He'd been undeniably bowled over by the sight of his friend in that hospital bed—which was the only reason she'd invited him to come back with her to the flat, she told herself. It was nothing at all to do with wanting him to be there... Not after the discovery she'd made in that elegant bathroom of his!

Neither of them seemed in a hurry to go back just yet, and presently they entered a small park and sat down on one of the unoccupied benches. As the day was beginning to draw to a close, most of the children had gone home but there were still one or two floating their boats on the pond, their parents casually reading the daily papers nearby. Giovanni stared at them pensively, his legs outstretched, his hands thrust into his pockets. He turned to glance at Emily.

'It always strikes me as strange that when something bad is happening in your own life, the lives of others go on uninterrupted,' he said quietly. 'Those people, those kids—they don't know about Rupert...what his parents are going through...'

Emily smiled and moved slightly closer to him. 'I do know what you mean, Giovanni,' she said softly. 'Ideally, we'd like everyone in the world to suffer at the same time as us, wouldn't we? It doesn't seem fair that they're not sharing the burden.'

He stared at her for a long moment. 'Exactly that,' he said. 'That's exactly what I was getting at.' He paused. 'Thanks for understanding,' he said. 'Thanks for not thinking me a complete idiot.'

Emily opened her bag to take out her mobile. 'I'll ring Coral,' she said, trying to inject a lighter note in her voice. 'To let her know there'll be three of us for dinner tonight.'

It was gone seven o'clock by the time they got home and Coral met them at the top of the stairs, her face flushed—either from cooking or from one or two pre-dinner drinks, Emily thought instinctively. Giovanni greeted her in his normal attentive way, but Emily was struck by his reticence, the unusual lack of unnecessary compliments.

'Giovanni,' Coral said, without waiting for anyone to say any more, 'I'm so sorry about your friend… How did you find him? Is he going to be OK?'

They all went inside and Giovanni explained the situation. 'So—apparently things may become clearer in forty-eight hours,' he said. 'It's a waiting game at the moment, I'm afraid.'

'Well, there's nothing more you can do now,' Coral said practically, 'and I always say, look on the bright side.' Goodness only knew she'd been trying to do that for the last month! 'And I'm already halfway through a good bottle of wine—so come on, help me finish it, Giovanni. It'll do you good. Then we'll have something to eat— there's nothing like a good meal to sustain you and, even if you don't feel like eating it, food always comforts the body and cheers the soul! Well, that's *my* theory.' She glanced up at him and Emily spotted the telltale signs on her friend's eager face—she was fascinated by him, as usual, by his overtly masculine persona.

Giovanni seemed more than ready to comply with her suggestion and in a few minutes he'd seated himself comfortably on the sofa, a drink in his hand, while Emily laid the small dining table with cutlery and glasses.

As she went into the kitchen, Coral caught her eye and raised hers extravagantly. 'He's *such* a dish,' she whispered, and Emily nudged her, a warning look on her face.

'All this looks good, Coral,' she said, loud enough for Giovanni to hear. 'Anything I can do—though it looks as if you've done it all anyway?'

'You can't, and I have,' Coral replied, shooing her away. 'Just open another bottle, Ellie.'

Later, with every scrap of food—including a mouth-watering crème brulée for pudding—having been consumed, they were sitting together in a semi-doze, sipping the last of the wine, when their front doorbell rang, bringing them out of their torpor for a second.

'I'll go,' Coral said without much enthusiasm, but Emily stood up at once.

'No, I'll get it,' and she left the room, going out into the tiny hallway. As she opened the door, she was surprised to see the owner of the flats standing there.

'Oh—Andy…' she began, and the man cut in apologetically.

'I'm really sorry to encroach on your Saturday evening, Emily,' he said, 'but I need to tell you about some new regulations regarding the properties—and I'll need your signature. Can you spare me a few minutes?' He paused. 'It's so difficult to find people in during the week—or indeed at any time,' he said, 'and I'm sorry to intrude.'

Emily smiled at him quickly. Andy Baker, a short middle-aged man with grey hair and a permanently worried expression on his face, was a very good landlord, always willing to sort out any complaint they might have.

'Of course I can spare you a few minutes, Andy,' she said, 'but we've got someone with us at the moment…' She paused. 'Look, I could pop upstairs to your place instead, if that's all right? It would probably be more convenient for you anyway, wouldn't it?'

'Oh, thanks, Emily…yes, of course.' He turned to go. 'It should only take us ten minutes to go through the stuff—more safety regulations, I'm afraid,' he added.

Back inside, Emily explained what it was all about.

'Sorry about this, Giovanni,' she said, 'but I shouldn't be long… Coral, make some coffee, will you, while I'm gone?' she added, thinking that it was time her friend diluted some of the alcohol she'd been drinking so freely.

Andy occupied the top flat of the four-floor dwelling, and Emily followed him up the stairs thinking how lucky she and Coral were to rent in the building, and to have Andy as their landlord. He never bothered them and was always businesslike in his dealings—and tonight was no exception as he showed Emily the several sheets of paper which she needed to study.

'And your signature here, Emily, please,' he said, 'and take this form with you so that Coral can add her signature as well. Any time will do. Just post it through my door at your convenience,' he added.

Well, that was painless enough, Emily thought as she went back downstairs.

As she'd followed Andy, she hadn't bothered to close their door properly behind her and, almost silently now, she went back into the flat to join the others, when, to her utter amazement, she saw that Coral had left her armchair to sit next to Giovanni on the sofa and was locked in what looked like a passionate kiss. And the worst of it was— Giovanni seemed to be thoroughly enjoying it!

'Am I interrupting something?' Emily asked coldly, trying to subdue the unreasonable feelings of resentment which had overtaken her with the force of an unexpected tidal wave. What Giovanni Boselli did—with Coral or anyone else he happened to be near—was nothing to her! It was surely what she might have expected, after all. Staring down at him, she could see that he was totally relaxed from enjoying their good food and wine, and now the bodily nearness of an all-too-available female was just what was needed to complete his pleasure. And he obviously was not going to pass up the opportunity. Did she need any further confirmation of her opinion of the man—and his compatriots? Easy come, easy go. Here today, gone tomorrow. She tried to swallow a painful lump in her throat—and failed miserably.

With a muffled screech, Coral pulled herself away and rose hurriedly to her feet, rushing past Emily and going into her bedroom, slamming the door behind her. Her sobbing was clearly audible and Emily stared down at Giovanni, who returned her gaze, his expression unfathomable.

'Well?' Emily demanded.

'Well, what?' Giovanni replied, apparently confused for a moment.

'Well, thanks for taking the first opportunity to…spread your favours around,' she began, and he raised his eyebrows in surprise.

'Does it matter to you, Emily?' he asked seriously.

'It matters that you took advantage of my friend while my back was turned!' she said hotly, suddenly realizing how that must sound. That she might be jealous!

He shrugged. 'I can only apologize,' he said casually. 'Especially after you've been good enough to show me such kindness and hospitality this evening…and spending some time with me today.' He paused for a long drawn-out moment. 'You must have a very low opinion of me, Emily,' he said quietly.

She looked back at him squarely, her eyes suspiciously moist. He was dead right, she thought—she did have a low opinion of him. And, at this moment, it couldn't possibly go much lower! Then she regained control of her feelings.

'It's of no consequence,' she said evenly. 'After all, it's a free world.'

After a few moments of uncomfortable silence, Giovanni moved across to stand close to her. He paused, hating the situation he was in and not being able to do anything about it. He looked down into her upturned, flushed features, longing to close his mouth over hers. Then, 'Can I ring you—as soon as I know more about Rupert…what his chances are?' he asked hesitantly, and Emily replied at once.

'Of course… I would *like* to know how he is,' she said, 'just as soon as you hear anything.' She paused. 'I'm spending tomorrow with my family, so I shan't be here, but you've got my mobile number.'

He nodded gravely, then left without another word and after he'd gone Emily stood alone in the room, trying to stop herself from bursting into tears. How could Coral have allowed him to do such a thing? To kiss her like that? After all…Giovanni was *her* friend, not Coral's!

# CHAPTER TEN

'DAD—your cooking is getting better all the time,' Emily said as she helped her father to load the dishwasher. 'I think you've been going to lessons and not telling us!'

Hugh Sinclair, a tall, handsome, rather spare-framed man with iron-grey hair and eyes to match, looked down at his daughter and smiled. 'Ah, well, I don't tell you everything, you know,' he said. 'But I'm glad you enjoyed it, Emily—and it's good to have a family to practice on.'

Together they took their coffee cups into the sitting room, where Paul was lounging on the sofa, idly turning the Sunday newspaper. Paul was a younger version of his father and, glancing at him fondly, Emily couldn't help wondering why he hadn't succumbed to the attentions of the women he came in contact with every day. She knew he'd had several girlfriends, and at least one serious relationship, but so far nothing had come of any of them.

'It says here,' Paul said, jabbing his finger at a page in front of him, 'that apparently we're all going to be living for ever. Medical science and high standards of living are going to ensure that it'll be the norm for everyone to reach one hundred and fifty, or even more. What do you think of that?'

Emily glanced at her father quickly. She knew that for a long while after the death of his wife he had not wanted to go on living at all…had told Emily, privately, that he didn't see the point now. And she'd tried to convince him that there was every point, that he was still loved and needed by his two children. She wondered what was going through his mind as he handed Paul his coffee. And his response to what Paul had said surprised her.

'Well, just so long as we can stay fit, mobile and in our right minds, I don't suppose that being one hundred and fifty will seem any different,' Hugh said. 'Just more of the same, though boredom may be the main adversary,' he added. 'I mean, how many more rounds of golf will it take to eventually cheese you off? Or how many more spring and summer plantings in the garden will finally get too much? Someone will have to invent other diversions.'

Emily looked at him as he stirred his coffee. His remarks were much more positive than she'd imagined they'd be… She might have expected him to say that he'd be happy to call it a day any time. In his darker moments, hadn't he told her that? But, after all, it was four years since the death of his wife. Perhaps time was doing its healing, after all, she thought.

Presently, sitting opposite his children, he looked at each of them in turn and cleared his throat. 'I'm glad you were both able to be here with me today,' he began, and immediately Emily put down her cup. Something in her father's voice alerted her sensitive intuition that there was something important coming…and she held her breath. Dad wasn't ill, surely? she thought, searching his face for telltale signs that something was wrong.

In his usual direct way, Hugh came straight to the point. 'You said you thought I'd been having cookery lessons,

Emily,' he said, 'and in a way I have been.' He paused. 'I've met someone called Alice who's been showing me a few tricks of the trade, so to speak… We met at the garden centre some time ago and got talking and, well, you know…she's in much the same position as me, and we've been kind of helping each other out with things now and again. I dug over a patch of garden for her earlier on, and helped her with some tax return stuff she didn't under-stand.'

For a moment there was complete silence as the others quickly put two and two together. Then Emily said slowly, 'You mean you have a…lady friend, Dad? Someone… special?' Even as she spoke the words, Emily could hardly believe it. Her father had always maintained that no one woman would ever—could ever—take the place of his adored wife…that he would never want another woman in his life. Yet he was several years off retirement age and still an attractive man…

Emily smiled a rather shaky smile. This was news indeed! 'Go on, Dad,' she said. 'Give us all the details.'

'Well, we've been seeing each other for about ten months,' Hugh replied slowly. 'Once or twice a week at first, then it became more frequent because Alice introduced me to her bridge-playing friends and we have regular card evenings…' He paused. 'I'm beginning to get the hang of it, but it's a fiendish game—mostly to do with being able to remember things—but it's very good for the brain-box, so they keep telling me.' He put down his cup. 'They're a great crowd, and I've been invited to one or two drinks evenings at their houses.' He glanced across at each of his children in turn. 'It's been very…pleasant…to be out and about with folk of my own age again, and to…have someone by my side. If you see what I mean,' he added quietly.

After her initial astonishment at this revelation, Emily felt a rush of warmth towards her father and, putting down her cup, she got up and went over to hug him.

'Dad, that's lovely—wonderful,' she said, smiling quickly. 'But…why haven't you told us before this? Why have you kept it to yourself all this time?' They had never been a secretive sort of family.

'Because for a long while I didn't think there was anything to tell,' Hugh said slowly. 'I didn't think our… friendship…was important, in that way.' He sighed. 'In today's language, I suppose you could say I was in denial. But I should have recognized my feelings sooner, admitted them.' He looked away for a moment. 'If I'd waited much longer I might have lost her.'

For the next few moments, the three of them stood with their arms wrapped around each other in mutual delight and understanding, with Hugh hugging his children so close they could hardly breathe. 'I was…worried that you might not approve…' he murmured and Emily held him away from her for a second.

'Dad,' she said softly, 'we only want what's best for you but…it all sounds rather serious—when are we going to be allowed to meet Alice?'

Hugh grinned, clearly relieved at the reception his news had received. 'Sooner than you might have thought,' he said mildly. 'She's coming over to have tea with us this afternoon.'

Much later, Paul walked Emily to the station to catch her train home. 'Well,' he said, looking down at his sister, 'I never expected to hear an announcement like that—did you? Good job I was sitting down at the time!'

Emily smiled happily. 'I'm delighted—for them both,'

she said. 'Wasn't Alice lovely? I know Mum would be happy for someone like her to keep Dad company.'

Paul was quiet for a moment, then, 'It's probably my own fault, but I have felt as if I've been in a kind of no-man's-land since Mum died,' he confessed. 'As if my own life has been on hold. But Dad's news frees me up to pursue some special plans of my own now…'

Emily stopped in her tracks. 'What? What's *this* all about?' she demanded. 'No more shocks today—please!'

'Oh, well, it's just that I've been given the chance to have a sabbatical for a year—to do some real travelling. Australia and New Zealand, for starters. You know it's been my ambition for some time, but I never felt I could leave Dad. He's not getting any younger.'

'Paul—that's brilliant!' Emily exclaimed, looking up at him eagerly. 'Will you go alone?'

'Not sure yet. Maybe, maybe not,' Paul answered, looking away.

'Hmm,' Emily murmured, deciding not to probe any further.

'Well, just let me point out that *you're* not getting any younger, either,' she said, 'so don't waste any more time— go ahead and spread your wings before they start to wither!'

'Thanks for the reminder,' Paul said drily, 'though I suppose I'll have to be prepared to fly home for the family wedding!'

Presently, as she sat in the train, Emily went over and over her father's news, admitting to feeling really surprised about it. Even though she was delighted for him, she'd never expected him to even consider the thought of another woman in his life—that that part of his existence was over. But…he'd obviously changed his mind, Emily thought pensively. A long-term single state was not for him, after all. She bit her lip. If her father could trust his life with someone again, perhaps there was hope that she, Emily, could do the same one day…

During the following week there was no message from Giovanni about Rupert, which didn't seem very optimistic and, although she was kept busy enough at work, Emily felt restless and on edge. The worst thing was, she and Coral had had a real showdown and she couldn't get it out of her mind. After hardly speaking to each other for a couple of days, everything had come out in a rush.

After a late-night shower, Coral had come into the sitting room where Emily was watching something on TV. 'I think we need to talk,' Coral had said, and Emily had immediately turned off the TV, looking up.

'I couldn't agree more,' she replied. 'Go on—enlighten me,' Emily said.

'I think you have a pretty good idea what I'm getting at,' Coral went on, and Emily frowned.

'I assure you, I have no idea at all.'

'Let's talk about our Italian friends, shall we…? Giovanni…and Nico? Remember Nico?'

Emily stood up, totally mystified. 'Who could ever forget Nico?' she said flatly.

'I surely don't need to spell it out!' Coral cried. 'He told me all about it, Ellie, how you were here together that evening and how you came on to him…almost begged him to make love to you! I mean, how do you think that made me feel? I would have trusted you with my life—never mind my boyfriend—and to say I was shattered is an understatement!'

Emily was transfixed by everything she was hearing. 'He…said…*what?*' she said unbelievingly.

'That you told him you'd always fancied him, and that you wanted him to…you know…'

Emily flopped her hands to her sides in complete resignation. 'Coral,' she said slowly, 'how could you believe such…such…total nonsense, such make-believe…such *lies*?' She shook her head slowly, while Coral looked across, her face flushed with emotion. 'Do you honestly think that I'd be capable of such a thing?' Emily paused. 'But I think you should know the truth. Nico was the guilty party in this case.' She hesitated, looking away for a second. 'I was in the kitchen, making us some tea, and he came in and almost trapped me against the sink—and I had to be really off with him, Coral. I didn't exactly tell him to get lost but it amounted to the same thing.' She paused, knowing that her heart rate had quickened at the memory of it all. 'I was never going to say a thing about it because it didn't matter. I was able to swat him like an irritating fly, and he got the message all right. But,' she added, 'I agonized over whether to tell you, to warn you, really, just what he's like.' She paused, reaching to put her hands on Coral's shoulders. 'I think you know that yourself. And I think you also know that I'd never betray you like that—we're mates, Coral. We do trust each other…don't we? Or I thought we did.'

In reply, Coral threw her arms around Emily's neck and held her tightly.

'Oh, Ellie,' she whispered, 'I'm sorry…really, I am.' She looked away for a moment. 'I'm really sorry I doubted you, even for a second, Ellie…and also that I…jumped on Giovanni on Saturday like that. I was only making a point, and I felt terrible afterwards. Disgusted with myself.'

The light suddenly began to dawn, and Emily whispered, 'You mean…Giovanni didn't…'

'He didn't do *anything*,' Coral sniffed. 'Of course, I'd had far too much to drink and I was grateful that he didn't try and push me off… Well, he's far too gallant for that, isn't he?' She blew her nose again. 'I was getting my own back on you, Emmy, that's all. Will you…forgive me?' she added.

Emily put her arms around Coral and held her tightly, suddenly feeling light-hearted—and light-headed. 'Of course I will, Coral,' she said, relieved, and embarrassed, by Coral's confession. Her own reaction at the time, and her attitude towards Giovanni, had spelt out its message all right. She did care about him! And she *was* jealous! She might just as well have shouted it from the rooftops!

Every time her mobile rang, Emily hoped that it would be some news about Rupert. Several times she'd been tempted to ring Giovanni herself, then decided against it. He had said he would get in touch if there was any change, and obviously there wasn't so it was better for her not to interfere. It wasn't as if she'd ever met Rupert, but Giovanni's haunted expression after he'd seen his friend would stay in her memory for a long time. The normal suave, somewhat devil-may-care confident manner had temporarily vanished, and it was obvious he'd been shattered by the appearance of his friend.

It wasn't until Thursday afternoon that Giovanni got in touch and at the sound of his voice Emily's heart leapt.

'Giovanni—I've been waiting for your call… How is…how is Rupert…?' She hardly dared to hear his answer, fearing the worst, but he cut in quickly.

'Rupert is going to be OK,' he said quietly. 'He regained full consciousness last night.' There was a long pause. 'They think he's going to pull through.'

Emily realized that her heart was pounding in her chest—this time with relief at the news—but why? she asked herself. Why did it matter so much to her, anyway? But of course she knew why. It was because she cared deeply about it for Giovanni's sake—and for Rupert's parents, of course—but mostly for Giovanni, whose obvious distress had upset her more than she wanted to admit, and whose happiness seemed to be more important to her than she'd imagined. Her voice was shaky as she answered.

'That's wonderful, Giovanni!' she exclaimed. 'Tell me everything. What caused his collapse? Was it…is it…?' She didn't want to frame the dreaded word.

There was silence for a moment. Then, 'Look, I can't tell you it all over the phone,' he said. 'I'm still at the hospital…but I'd love to see you, Emily. Can you meet me somewhere this evening?' As he spoke, Giovanni crossed his fingers. He'd expected a frosty reception to his call, and was massively relieved that Emily seemed her normal self.

'Of course I can!' Emily said at once. 'Oh, Giovanni, I'm so happy for you—for Rupert and his parents… They must be ecstatic. I was so…so afraid when there was no news…'

'So were we all,' he replied grimly.

Emily thought quickly. She didn't want to suggest that Giovanni came to the flat again.

'Giovanni, let's meet by the river,' she said, 'down by the London Eye. About seven-thirty? We could have a drink or a coffee somewhere.'

'OK, fine,' he agreed.

By the time Emily had finished everything she had to do at the office it was gone six-thirty and she knew she'd have to hurry if she wasn't to keep Giovanni hanging around waiting for her. Downstairs in the cloakroom, she changed into a pretty pink dress. Then, after a wash and touching up her make-up, she brushed her hair and tied it back in a long ponytail. Glancing at herself in the long mirror so thoughtfully provided by the management, she wondered why her appearance mattered…but she knew the answer to that. It mattered because she was going to be with Giovanni Boselli. She wanted him to like what he saw, and she stared at her reflection for a moment. She'd never intended for this to happen, had never intended that the unlooked-for relationship should deepen at all—but somehow it had started to and she seemed powerless to stop it. Then she shook her head, cross with herself. What she did, or didn't do, was entirely up to her and she could find plenty of good reasons not to see him ever again—if that was what she wanted.

She turned away resolutely and left the building. The only reason she was seeing Giovanni now was to let him tell her all about his friend—who, thankfully, was going to recover. So that particular panic was over.

She was almost twenty minutes late before she got to the Eye, and she spotted him at once—at the same time that he saw her tripping down the steps towards him. Walking swiftly to meet her, his smile broadened and he caught her hand in his, looking down at her approvingly.

'It's so good to see you, Emilee-a,' he murmured. 'I've booked us a short trip on the water… It's such a lovely evening. I hope that's OK?'

'Perfectly OK,' Emily replied. She loved a boat trip, and it would be a wonderfully relaxing way to sit and talk for an hour, she thought.

Still holding her hand tightly, he led her over to the moorings and helped her onto the boat, which was waiting.

There were only a handful of people already aboard and, pushing her gently in front of him, Giovanni indicated one of the seats at the back. Then he sat next to her and looked down, resting his arm across her shoulders. And Emily looked up into those mesmerizing eyes, feeling her whole body flood with an indescribable heat, making her almost breathless. Swallowing quickly, she turned away, watching the boat being untied, watching as the water began to move alongside them, watching the gulls soar hopefully. Eventually, Giovanni broke the silence between them.

'Thanks for postponing whatever else you had planned for tonight, Emily,' he said softly, and she interrupted.

'I wasn't doing anything,' she said. She paused. 'And I do want to hear about Rupert.' She hesitated, thinking that now was not the moment to mention Saturday night, if she could ever bring herself to do it. 'I thought you were never going to ring. As each day passed I thought the worst must have happened,' she said.

He tightened his hold on her. 'Yes—sorry I didn't get in touch, but there was nothing to say… All the waiting, watching, hoping, despairing…was awful, Emily. Like a nightmare.'

'Were you there all the time?' Emily asked.

'Yes, almost,' he replied. 'I felt I couldn't leave Rupert's parents to shoulder it alone… They seemed to gain strength from me being there.' He paused, swallowing, and, looking up quickly, Emily could see that he still seemed moved by the experience.

Then, little by little, all the details came out—how the three at the bedside had talked quietly about old times, funny things they remembered, new plans, new hopes, anything and everything to help pass the hours. How, once or twice, Rupert had seemed to come round, then would sink back to the oblivion which enveloped him. And, as Giovanni spoke, Emily leaned into him—as if she wanted to share the crisis—and the feel of her soft body melting so deliciously into his provoked such an intense desire in Giovanni that he had difficulty in restraining himself, in not telling her how much he desired her, longed for her, wanted her for ever.

Pulling himself together, he stared down at the water beneath them for a few seconds. 'Have you noticed how distant all the traffic seems, even though we're still in the middle of town?' he murmured.

'Yes,' Emily said. 'Any expanse of water has the effect of isolating you, doesn't it?' She paused. 'But—go on—about Rupert…'

Giovanni took a deep breath. 'Well, the breakthrough came last night,' he said. The nurses had made their final rounds and I was preparing to go back to my hotel. Rupert's mother was going to have a couple of hours' sleep in the side room while his father was going to stay up and keep watch.' Giovanni swallowed, and some-thing—she didn't know what—made Emily rest her head on his shoulder, turning her face into his neck, his dark masculine scent making her body churn.

'Go on,' she said quietly.

Headily conscious, now, of Emily's action, Giovanni waited a few seconds, not wanting to interrupt the moment. Then, 'I was bending slightly over Rupert, squeezing his hand…and…you know…saying, "G'night, mate—see you tomorrow"…and suddenly his eyes opened, almost lazily, you'd say, and he said…he said…'

'Go on,' Emily murmured, looking up into Giovanni's eyes, which were wet with tears. 'What else?'

'Rupert looked straight at me and said, "Joe—Lucky Joe—what are *you* doing here?"'

Recalling the event, Giovanni couldn't go on for a second, and Emily squeezed his hand, swallowing a lump in her own throat. What a moment that must have been! For Rupert, for his parents—and for Giovanni! That he should be the first whom Rupert had responded to!

Releasing her hand briefly, Emily took a tissue from her bag and touched Giovanni's wet cheeks, and he didn't stop her. Seeing him emotionally upset did not detract in any way from Giovanni's masculinity, she thought. And it was nothing less than she would have expected from a passionate Italian male. It was part of his strength.

'So,' she said, 'what now?'

'Well, there is still a long way to go,' Giovanni said, 'but our worst fears are over, and Rupert's basically a strong man... They're sure he'll pull through, though it's bound to take time. But, as his mother said—when she'd stopped dancing around the place—we've got all the time in the world. And anything precious is worth waiting for.'

Sitting there together on the gently chugging boat, with occasional lights beginning to come on along the riverbank, there didn't seem any need to say much more at that moment...Giovanni revelling, not only in his good news, but in being clasped in Emily's soft arms. Because she had responded to him in the way he was used to with women...in the last half an hour he felt that a massive emotional barrier between them had been breached, and if his luck held he may still be in with a chance.

And Emily, with her head tucked into his neck, could only wonder at this man she was nestling into. At what a valued, loyal friend he must be to those he loved—and how disarmingly vulnerable he himself could be. Not mention those other things—drop-dead good looks, a physique to make the mouth water and a sensuous tenderness to warm the coldest heart. So then—what of her good intentions? She mustn't let him get to her like this… Wasn't Giovanni Boselli the enticing chocolate that could have poison at its centre?

And then, unbelievably and almost in slow motion and as if it was the most natural thing in the world, Giovanni took her into his arms properly, turning her so that they embraced as two lovers, his arms encasing her soft body and his dark head bent to reach her mouth. And, without stopping to think, Emily responded eagerly, loving the feel of him, the feel of his body harden against hers, the intoxicating sensuousness of their moist parted lips melding as one. Her whole body throbbed with desire, every warning instinct flying away with the breeze as he slipped his hand inside her dress and held her breast in his palm. Her flesh yielded to the magical press of his fingertips and she had difficulty in controlling her breathing.

How long they remained there like that, neither would ever know. What they did know was that they both wished it could go on for ever, where nothing could interrupt this time of gentle lovemaking or break the delight of unexpected passion.

Presently, Emily regained something of her self-control and sat back, pushing a wisp of hair away from her face. And, easing himself away, Giovanni looked down at her, his eyes black with continuing desire for this beguiling woman. He cleared his throat.

'I could do with a drink,' he said huskily, 'and isn't it time for some food?' Though food was the last thing on his mind! 'We're almost back where we started from,' he added, 'so we'll be getting off in a few minutes.'

'I know somewhere nearby where they do good snacks,' Emily said, 'then I must go home, Giovanni...'

'Of course,' he replied, 'and it was good of you to meet me tonight, Emily. I appreciate it.' She'd never know *how* much!

By now it was getting dark and the lights of the city had come on, casting gentle shafts of gold into the night sky. Not daring to glance at herself in her handbag mirror, Emily wondered whether all the erotic feelings which had engulfed her were written all over her features! But she did not regret the experience, not for a single second... Giovanni was the very first Italian she'd ever known in a close sense—and all she could think was *Wow!* She couldn't begin to imagine what might have followed in a more private situation...!

They disembarked and found the place to eat and presently, as they sat with their coffee, he said casually, 'By the way, I have a very special invitation for you, Emilee-a,' and she looked up at him quickly. 'My dear Mamma is going to be sixty in October,' he went on, 'and there is to be a big party.' He paused, looking across at her, melting her heart with his gaze. 'Please say you will come, Emily. I will take you. We will go together.'

Emily couldn't help smiling. She'd not expected *that* kind of invitation. Not so soon after meeting Giovanni's mother. 'When is it to be?' she asked.

'On the twenty-eighth—I hope you are free,' he said earnestly.

'Well, I'll have to look at my diary,' she said, knowing very well that she was not booked up that month. 'But thank you for inviting me,' she added politely.

She smiled up at him. She'd have to think of something a really good excuse not to accept, she thought, after wha had happened to her on the boat earlier. Her common sense was trying to tell her something! He was alluring, she admitted that, and, heaven help her, she could begin to adore him! But her deep anxiety of not being able to trust would just not leave her... No, she would not be going to Italy with Giovanni Boselli for his mother's party, or for any other reason. Definitely, definitely not!

# CHAPTER ELEVEN

AFTER what could only be described as an incident-packed week, Emily decided that, so far as relationships were concerned, she was going to have a complete rest and not think about anyone at all for a bit. Rupert's predicament, her father's announcement, Coral's confession and, most of all, her heated moments with Giovanni on the boat, must all be pushed into the background of her thoughts.

But the rest she'd promised herself was short-lived when one morning she received a call on her mobile and, hearing Coral's voice, she frowned briefly. The two girls rarely contacted each other during office hours.

'Coral, hi—what is it?'

'You'll never guess, Ellie. Steve's just called me, and he sounded awful! Said he had to see me.' There was a pause. 'Something's wrong, I know it is…I think he may be ill!'

Emily smiled briefly. Coral was such a softie, she thought—even after the casual, heartless way Steve had dropped her, she still cared about him. 'Well, what else did he say?' Emily asked.

'Not much—just that he had a big problem and needed to see me about it. Do…do you think I should see him, Ellie, talk to him?'

'I suppose there can be no harm in doing that, Coral,' Emily said guardedly. 'But, you know, keep things casual.' The memory of how hurt and upset her friend had been was still uppermost in Emily's mind.

They rang off and Emily sat staring into space for a few moments. The way that Steve had behaved had been so out of character it had completely shattered Coral—and mystified Emily. He was a decent, kind man—or so she'd always thought. How could he have changed overnight and been so cruel? Then her mouth tightened. Hadn't she been dealt the same kind of blow herself? Why should anyone be surprised by anything, or anyone? People did change, she thought bitterly, even the ones you least expected to. No wonder you had to be wary of the opposite sex—of people in general.

Although her curiosity about Steve's phone call was killing her, Emily decided not to contact Coral later in the day. Anyway, they were hectic again at work, which more than occupied her mind. It was seven-thirty before she got home and, unusually, Coral was there first.

'Well?' Emily said at once. 'How did it go—what's the matter with Steve?'

'He's asked me to forgive him, wants to know whether we can get back on track.'

This was news indeed! As far as Emily knew, there'd not even been a phone call since the split. 'I don't…believe… it,' she said slowly. 'What did you say to him?'

'Well, my first instinct was to say that I'd have to give it a great deal of thought,' Coral said, 'but I couldn't do that, Ellie. Because all I wanted was to put my arms around his neck and hug him, tell him it would be all right—that we could make it all OK.' She shook her head slowly. 'You know, I've never stopped loving him, not really. I tried to hate him, and for a while I think I did, but when all is said and done we go back too far. And he said he was sorry so many times, over and over again, that I had to tell him to stop.'

'He *was* the one at fault,' Emily reminded her gently.

'In the sense that he was the one who did the dumping,' Coral admitted. 'But there's more to it than that, Ellie.' She hesitated. 'I was more than half to blame—I did some-times take Steve for granted, began to treat him like a con-venient sort of. .well…friend. Knew he'd always be there, be the same, so our whole relationship became rather mundane.' She got up and went over to the window. 'Last year he wanted us to be more committed to each other—to get engaged—and I put him off.'

'Why—why did you do that?' Emily asked. 'Were you having doubts?'

'No—no, of course not,' Coral replied. 'It was because… because it was just at the time that Marcus—you and Marcus—finished.' She turned to glance at Emily. 'How would you have felt with me flashing an engagement ring in your face? So I told Steve there was no hurry, and we could wait a bit. And then, somehow, we just went on as before.'

Emily was horrified to think that her problems had upset things. 'You shouldn't have turned Steve down, Coral,' she said slowly. 'Not for my sake. It could have been the worst mistake you'd made in your life.'

Coral's face broke into a wide grin. 'Well, I don't think so,' she said. 'We sat in that bar today, holding hands and looking at each other like a pair of love-struck teenagers…. He's my sort…that's all there is to it. And I was happy to tell him that.'

Emily breathed a long sigh of relief—and happiness for Coral. In her opinion, she and Steve had been like a pigeon-

pair from the word go—that was why it had been so stagger-
ing when they'd parted. She went over to Coral and hugged
her. 'So—you've obviously forgiven him,' she said teasingly.

'We've forgiven each other,' Coral said simply. 'But
we're not rushing things.'

'Very wise,' Emily said.

'No—we're going to take it easy—for at least the
next week!'

Two weeks later, Giovanni arrived back in London, his
longing to see Emily again almost overwhelming. It was
Monday morning and he knew she'd be in the office…
unless they'd sent her somewhere abroad. He kept his
fingers crossed against that possibility as he waited for her
to answer her mobile, and the sound of her voice sent his
spirits soaring. She was in England—and only a ten
minute walk away!

'Emilee-a,' he said breathily and, despite having given
herself a good talking-to all the time they'd been apart,
Emily felt a surge of excitement as she heard him.

'Oh…Giovanni…' she began. 'You're back.' Well, he'd
told her what his plans were on the phone a couple of days
ago. He'd been ringing her frequently while he was back
in Italy, keeping her up to date with Rupert's progress and
other less important things, and each time Emily had
managed to keep their conversations brief—either saying
she was busy or just going out or just getting into the
shower—any excuse not to let that seductive voice knock
her off balance. And Giovanni was well aware what was
going on… They were playing a discreet cat and mouse
game, this woman and him—and the only effect her
attitude had was to make him double his efforts, increase
his determination to capture this provocative female,

because he knew he wanted her more than anything else he'd ever wanted in his life. He had this instinctive feeling that they could be sublimely happy together… He knew he would love her for ever and could make her happy. All he had to do was convince her of the fact. And to make her love him.

'I certainly am back,' he said, 'to find plenty of work here waiting for me.'

'Your time is going to be precious, then,' she began, and he cut in.

'There will always be time to speak to a beautiful woman,' he said.

'And I'm sure there are plenty of those near you right now,' she said lightly.

'Hmm. Not so you'd notice,' he replied, thinking that there wasn't a woman within a mile who could compete with Emily. He hesitated, but only for a second. 'Can I see you tonight?'

Emily bit her lip. She'd tried to cool her feelings for Giovanni during the time he'd been back in Italy, had made a determined effort to keep busy with other things, other thoughts. She and Coral had managed to give the flat a good clean—something which didn't often happen, she admitted, because they never seemed to be there together long enough with the time to do it. Emily had also started on another painting—although that didn't always stop her thinking. In fact, it was often the perfect opportunity for introspection and, as she'd worked her brush delicately over the canvas, her mind had been constantly tormented by the recollection of those few moments on the river. Giovanni's magnetic animal energy as his lips had locked onto hers, the demonstration of his physical need for her, had shaken her equilibrium. And the short-lived incident

had left her vulnerable and open, hinting as it did of un-
dreamed-of passion. She knew that, despite all her reservations, she was longing for something else, something
even more beautiful with Giovanni. She had been kissed
many, many times before, but not like that. It was the air
of breathless intensity enveloping them which had excited
her beyond all imagining. *How* was this all going to end?
she asked herself hopelessly. How could she end it?

'Um…sorry, I'm busy tonight,' she murmured in answer
to his request. 'I've promised to help Coral with something.'

There was a pause. 'Oh, well, never mind,' Giovanni
said, clearly disappointed to be turned down. 'But are you
going to be busy every evening? Can I see you tomorrow
or Wednesday?' He'd wait for ever, if necessary, he
thought grimly.

'Well, OK—Wednesday, then,' Emily said, trying not
to sound hard-to-get, even though that was her intention.
She could not be ungracious or unkind. He didn't deserve
that. But how could she make him get the message that she
was afraid to trust him? Or that she wouldn't be prepared
to share him with any passing female who crossed his
path? Her eyes hardened as she remembered that seductive negligee hanging up in his bathroom. 'Shall we meet
outside my office at six-thirty?' she said briskly. 'Will you
have finished work by then?'

'Wednesday at six-thirty,' he agreed at once. 'I can tell
you all the plans for my mother's surprise party,' he added.

Emily shut her mobile and stared out of the window for
a moment. Of course, that party. Now he was going to
involve her properly, make her part of this family occasion,
draw her in like a fish on a hook. Sighing deeply, she picked
up her lists and started to type. She was not going to Italy,

she thought, to a party or to anything else. Not with Giovanni Boselli. No, no, no. It would just prolong the agony.

On the Saturday evening three weeks later, Giovanni drove slowly along the winding drive which led to the imposing building set into the gently sloping hillside. Emily caught her breath as she gazed in awe. She'd had no idea of exactly what Giovanni's family home might look like, and what she was seeing took her completely by surprise. The setting was spectacular enough, but the dwelling itself was magnificent to look at, its creamy high stone walls glinting in the rapidly setting sunlight and surrounded by acres of private olive groves. Emily looked across at Giovanni as he brought the car to a standstill outside the huge pillared entrance.

'Is this…is this really your "place in the country"?' she asked. 'Or are we just passing through?'

He looked back at her, his dark eyes unusually thoughtful, and his voice as he answered held a trace of caution. 'Well, yes, this is the family bolt-hole,' he said briefly. 'The one I've always looked upon as my home.'

The 'family bolt-hole!' Emily thought. It was a palace—by anyone's standards! She took a deep breath. 'It's fantastic, Giovanni,' she said softly. 'Why would you want to live anywhere else in the whole world?'

He smiled quizzically at that. 'Come on,' he said. 'You're probably tired and looking forward to dinner. I told them when to expect us.'

They got out of the car and went up the stone steps into the massive tile-floored entrance hall. The tall shuttered windows all around led Emily's stupefied gaze to the vaulted ceiling above and she had difficulty in keeping her jaw from dropping as she took it all in. This was the home of *very* wealthy owners, she thought. Giovanni had never even hinted at such prosperity.

Just then a pretty Italian woman approached them and Giovanni said, 'Ah, Rosa—this is Emily. Would you show her where she's going to be sleeping, please?'

'Of course, Giovanni,' the woman said, gazing up into his eyes in the sort of way that spaniels did to their owners. She smiled at Emily, taking her small case from her and ushering her towards the wide curved stone staircase. So there was staff in attendance, too, Emily thought—but anywhere this size would certainly need it!

Alone, Emily stared around the large room she'd been allocated, then went slowly across to the window, whose shutters were wide open, allowing her a breathtaking view of the scene in front of her. In the distance was the uninterrupted countryside, and surrounding the house were serried ranks of olive trees and grapevines. Almost directly below her window was the swimming pool. It was flanked by a series of bay trees and tubs of flowers and generously supplied with sun loungers, wooden tables and chairs and umbrellas—though these were closed now and the October air felt distinctly chilly as Emily turned away thoughtfully.

Someone had already switched on the lamps by the side of the double bed and, as Emily slowly unpacked the few things she'd brought with her for the weekend, she felt somehow uneasy—and distinctly irritated. In falling in—reluctantly, and after much persuasion—with Giovanni's insistence that she should come to this event, she felt she'd been caught on the wrong foot. Why hadn't she been given some idea of the sort of place she'd be coming to? Who else would be coming to the party, had she brought the right dress to wear—would she fit in with the obviously moneyed gathering? Emily cringed as she thought of her humble little flat, how Giovanni had sat at the minute dining table. His place in Rome had been fantastic enough—goodness only knew—but this was something else! And had he deliberately not told her about it to impress her? To sweep her off her feet? Because it certainly seemed like that to Emily. He'd never given her any idea of the opulence of his family home. Were they aristocracy, the Boselli family? Was there an illustrious Count somewhere amongst their forebears?

She finished unpacking her case and laid out her clothes anxiously. This evening was no problem—because she'd been told that it was to be just her and Giovanni here—so her cream trousers and purple shirt would do, she thought, though she knew she'd be glad of her favourite go-anywhere wrap later. It had been a birthday present from her father a couple of years ago, and Emily knew it had cost him a great deal of money because stitched in one corner was the tiny revealing logo of the famous fashion house that had designed it. The fabric was of sheer fine wool, with a pearl background and narrow, pale, multi-shaded stripes. And, delicately hinting at every colour in the rainbow, it always teamed happily with everything Emily wore.

But as for tomorrow night's big party—the one which Maria, apparently, wasn't aware of—Emily hoped that the dress she'd brought would be suitable for the occasion. It certainly wasn't new because she'd only agreed to come here two days ago, and there'd been no time to go shopping for something else. It was a raw silk number in a luminous jewel-green, low-necked and with a three-quarter length hemline. Its exquisite, simple cut and shape was perfect to display Emily's dainty waist and hips and, as she hung it carefully on a hanger, she couldn't help smiling to herself. It was the only designer dress she'd ever bought—or was ever likely to buy, she thought—and the only person who knew the charity shop it had come from was Coral, who'd promised not to tell. Admiring it again, Emily wondered who else had owned it—and why they'd not kept it for ever... Maybe the wearer had put on some weight! Well, *she'd* never get rid of it, she thought as she went into the bathroom. Anything of that quality should be cherished.

Presently, there was a discreet knock on the door. Giovanni stood outside. 'Everything OK, Emily?' he asked, glancing down at her, his eyes softening. She always looked so good, he thought instinctively. 'Have you everything you need?' he enquired.

Together, they went down the staircase and Giovanni said, 'We'll have dinner on the patio—they've put the heaters outside...' He cupped his hand under her elbow as they negotiated the last few steps, and Emily looked up at him.

'Where is Maria tonight?' she asked curiously. So far, she'd only met Rosa.

'She's being entertained to dinner by some friends,' he said briefly.

As they sat at a table on the patio a stout Italian woman appeared with wine in an ice bucket. She smiled cheerfully at Emily as she put it down in front of Giovanni, who immediately started to uncork the bottle. He introduced them casually.

'This is Emily,' he said, glancing up, 'and this is our irreplaceable Margherita, Emily, who's been keeping us all too well fed for as long as I can remember.'

Margherita raised her eyes extravagantly at Emily, murmuring *'Allora,'* before departing to bring in their dinner.

Presently, after they'd eaten the delicious meal, Giovanni poured their coffee and glanced briefly across at Emily, who he'd been aware was unusually quiet this evening.

'Is anything wrong, Emilee-a?' he asked. 'Are you feeling OK?'

Emily looked back at him steadily. 'I'm feeling perfectly well, thanks,' she said, 'but slightly confused, that's all.' She paused, trying to find the right words. 'I had no idea of the sort of place I'd been invited to and…it's taken me by surprise.'

Giovanni sighed and leaned back in his chair. 'Yes, I know…I apologize, Emily,' he said slowly. 'But it's very difficult to explain to people. Well, let's say I always find it difficult,' he added. Emily raised her eyebrows as he went on slowly, 'Do you know…have you heard of the Antonio chain?'

Interrupting him, Emily answered at once. 'You mean *the* Antonio…the famous couturiers?' she said. 'But of course I have.' Every woman knew the company whose modern but untrendy designs were coveted by thousands of devoted clients.

'Well—that's us. That's the family. The business—and the burden.' He waited a moment before going on. 'It all began a long time ago with my great-grandfather, Antonio, who was not only a talented artist but also a shrewd businessman, and he had the good sense to fall in love with, and marry, an accomplished seamstress.' He paused. 'Like many successful companies, it started in a very small way, with just the two of them to begin with, but it grew steadily over the years, becoming what it is today.' Giovanni drank from his cup, not looking at Emily, who was in a state of mild shock as she took in what he'd said. Antonio was best known for the quality of fabrics they worked with, together with their unique simplicity of style—and prices which were not totally out of the question for those with a steady income.

'Strangely enough,' Giovanni went on, putting down his cup, 'we have not been very successful on the family front. Antonio had two sons—one of whom died young, which eventually left my grandfather and his wife to carry the baton. Then they produced my father and his brother, Aldo—but, as you know, my father, too, died far too young, leaving me virtually holding the reins—with my dear Mamma very much in the front seat, of course.' He smiled.

'What's happened between you and Aldo?' Emily asked bluntly, feeling that she was entitled to ask whatever questions she liked.

Giovanni pursed his lips. 'A few years ago, Aldo acted shamefully…very dishonourably…over a certain matter with a competitor. There was great deal of harm done at the time,' he added. 'Our small team of directors wanted to vote him off, and out, but…I…persuaded them that Aldo was still part of the bloodline and that he should stay and be paid a small salary, and the firm pays his children's school fees. He only plays a nominal part in the business now, and has little say in important decisions. Anyway—' Giovanni shrugged '—I suppose it's inevitable that Aldo should resent me because my father left all his possessions to me, making me the majority shareholder. So what I say goes.'

'Where does everything all happen?' Emily asked curiously. 'Where is the factory, the workshops…?'

'Oh, well, in the very early days it actually functioned from here, from this place,' Giovanni said, 'but for many years we've rented design and factory space in the industrial estate outside Rome. There's plenty of room for everyone there.'

Emily sat with her hands in her lap and looked across at Giovanni. 'But…why all the secrecy?' she asked. 'Why wait until now before letting me know what company I've been keeping lately?' She shook her head briefly. 'Shall I drop a deep curtsy—or provide a roll of drums?' she added sarcastically.

Giovanni almost shouted in response. 'No! That is just the point, Emily! Oh… It is so much worse having to admit to a rich dynasty than to admit to having nothing! What should I say to anyone? *Hi, I'm Giovanni Boselli and I'm part of the Antonio fashion chain and I've inherited its fortune—plus the responsibility of carrying it on for the rest of my life.'*

Giovanni's handsome features were flushed under his dark skin as he spoke. 'It is very difficult for me, as a man meeting new friends who might…' and Emily interrupted before he could go on.

'Oh, I get it!' she said hotly. 'Beware of gold-digging females, is that it, Giovanni? Well! I'm surprised that it's taken you all this time to realize that I couldn't care *less* what you own, or who you are, or what your background is!' Emily felt her anger rising with every second that passed, and now Giovanni half stood up, leaning across the table to put his face closer to hers.

'It took me no time at all to know what sort of woman you are, Emily,' he said harshly, 'but I have been wrong… hurt…disenchanted…before. And I have hurt other people, too. It is so…difficult.' He sat down again heavily, and went on more quietly. 'I have been so sure of you, so *re*assured, from almost the first moment I met you, and yes, while I'm on the subject, I *do* believe in love at first sight, because I love you, Emily, more deeply than I can express…and don't look at me like that, because I mean every word of what I'm saying! But I wanted to make *you* love *me*—if that were possible—for *myself.* And for no other reason. I wanted you to love me, like me, want to be with me as much as I want to be with you. And for nothing—*nothing*—to get in our way, in the way of our happiness.' He paused for a moment, gazing at Emily with such uninhibited ardour that it made her senses reel. He was sweeping her off her feet—making her feel dizzy. And, in spite of all her reservations, she knew that she could be in imminent danger of admitting her love for him, too! She'd been trying to deny her feelings for weeks, trying to talk herself out of wanting to be near him, and it had been getting more difficult with each day that passed.

Shakily, she picked up her coffee and sipped for a moment, knowing that he was waiting for some response from her, but, despite the obvious sincerity of his words, Emily felt ruffled and hurt. He had been testing her, judging her all this time, sizing her up—presumably as a possible wife! That made her feel small and silly. She stared across at him, her mind so churned up with a myriad emotions she thought she was going to be sick. Why had she agreed to come here this weekend? All her instincts had warned her against it—but Giovanni Boselli was used to getting what he wanted. She took a deep breath, trying to calm down. She was here now—nothing could alter that— and she wouldn't embarrass everyone—embarrass herself— by sulking or being difficult. She wouldn't spoil Maria's party. But she still wasn't sure how to handle this, how to handle Giovanni and what he'd just told her. It was all too much—much too much.

'I think I must go to bed now, Giovanni,' she said slowly. 'Do you mind if we continue our…discussion… some other time?'

Much later the following evening, after an amazing display of fireworks had concluded the festivities and the last guest had departed, Emily stood alone in her room, her head bursting. She'd never before been to a party like it!

Earlier in the day Giovanni had taken his mother and Emily out for a long drive, taking them miles into the countryside, ostensibly for a relaxing time in remote villages to browse, and to have coffee and lunch. And when they'd arrived back home just before seven o'clock, what a sight had met their eyes! The place had been transformed into a film set! Coloured lights had swayed from every tree, huge displays of fresh flowers graced every corner of the huge patio, and already masses of people— all beautifully dressed for the occasion—had gathered around, waiting to greet Maria. Emily had wondered whether Maria would be overwhelmed by this totally unexpected celebration, but from the expression in her eyes as she'd hugged her son excitedly and then went on to embrace all her friends, no one need have worried. Maria had been in her element.

Presently, Emily and Maria had gone upstairs to their rooms to change before soon rejoining the gathering outside. A small band had already taken up position on an elevated corner of the area and soon medleys of current popular songs had added to the noisy gaiety, while uniformed caterers moved among the crowd with trays of mouth-watering canapés. There were so many guests, more arriving every few minutes, that Emily had difficulty keeping up with it all, and it was hard for Giovanni to be everywhere at once, though he had introduced her to as many people as he could. Left by herself for a moment, Emily had searched around the milling crowds, hoping to see that beautiful face in the photograph somewhere, that special someone, but she couldn't spot her anywhere. But—she *had* to be one of the guests, surely, the girl had thought... It stood to reason.

Now, before she got ready for bed, Emily took from her case the daintily wrapped present she'd brought for Maria—who'd received so many presents at the party tonight she must have lost count, the girl thought—but Emily had decided she'd wait until tomorrow, Monday, the actual birthday, before giving it to her. She bit her lip thoughtfully, hoping it would be deemed good enough for Maria. The woman's other gifts would have been fabulously expensive, judging by the obviously wealthy guests. The present Emily was holding in her hand was one of her own small framed water-colours, and it pictured a goose leading a line of tiny goslings along a wooded path towards a pond in the background. She smiled now, as she remembered the occasion when she and Coral had come across the little feathered family. It had been on a warm afternoon out that they'd enjoyed together a year ago, and Emily had committed the scene to memory before getting around to painting it. And, unusually for her, she had been pleased with the result.

Slowly, she undressed and got into bed, thinking what a strange day it had been. Surreal, almost. She had spent the entire time with Giovanni, yet neither of them had referred to their conversation of last night. Well, Maria had been there too, which of course would have made it difficult but, even so, it was almost as if their discussion hadn't taken place. Every now and then she caught Giovanni looking at her, but she deliberately didn't want to catch his eye… She still felt totally bewildered at being here with this family—this renowned family--with its fabulously rich heir apparently wanting to make her part of it…and she still couldn't get her head around it all. He had said, with such conviction, that he *loved* her… But Marcus had been good at that kind of thing, too, she remembered. She turned over impatiently. She shouldn't have agreed to come. She should have listened to her inner self.

Later, much later, Emily drew herself up to a sitting position in quiet desperation. At this rate, she was *never* going to get to sleep, she thought, as she rested her head on her bent knees for a moment. She seemed to have been tossing and turning for ever. Everything that had gone on during the party, the loud conversation all around, the in-sistent beat of the music, the shrieks of uninhibited laughter and the general carnival atmosphere which Italians seemed so good at enjoying, had left Emily wide awake. Not to mention everything Giovanni had said to her when they'd been alone. But the eerie silence now, after all the noise, was making it worse… Was everyone else in the whole world fast asleep? If so, why wasn't she?

She switched on the lamp beside her and glanced at her watch. Three o'clock! Still a long time to go before morning. Getting out of bed, she went across to the bathroom and poured herself a glass of water. Well, that might go some way towards eradicating the effect of all the champagne she'd had.

She took a long drink, then, after a moment, went over to the window and quietly drew back the shutters, gazing out at the now familiar scene. It was simply perfect here she thought, the now subdued lighting casting stran shadows all around, the water in the pool moving gently as the breeze ruffled its surface. Emily took in all the details in her usual observant way… One day, she might like to paint all that she was seeing.

Suddenly, her attention was caught by the sight of two figures strolling onto the patio, their arms entwined, their faces close together, and Emily hurriedly drew back… It was Giovanni and that woman! The woman in the picture! It just had to be—even though in the dim light it was hard to be certain… But, yes, it *was* her…and she was looking up at Giovanni, who was murmuring softly into her ear, his lips caressing her face in the sort of intimate, unhurried manner of an attentive lover.

Emily's mouth had gone completely dry as she stood unashamedly watching them, and she realized that her legs were trembling slightly. But why? Wasn't this to be expected? These two were well-known to each other—very well-known! And what difference did it make to her, anyway? It just proved what she'd known all along—Giovanni Boselli liked women, full stop! And in the plural! Emily suddenly felt a wave of anger engulf her as she continued watching… Now the two were sitting, half concealed by a large shrub, but what they were doing was clear enough! The woman's head was resting on Giovanni's shoulder and he was holding her tenderly…whispering so tenderly…and, with a start of genuine surprise, Emily knew that she was feeling upset and jealous! *Jealous* of a two-timing character she wouldn't trust as far as she could throw! The man who only a few hours ago had professed his love for *her,* Emily Sinclair! Had given her all that drivel about wanting to make her love him as much as he loved *her!* Well, he must think she was born yesterday!

She stood back and closed the shutters softly, only just

stopping herself from bursting into tears. What the hell was the matter with her? *She* didn't want Giovanni, no thank *you!* So why was she feeling so…so…completely bewildered—and so devastated?

# CHAPTER TWELVE

WHEN she woke the following morning, Emily felt tired and dispirited. If only she were home now, she thought, in their unprepossessing little flat that had no marble staircases or swimming pools or olive groves—and no Giovanni Boselli, either.

But she still had almost a day to get through before their flight, a day in which she must appear normal and friendly and happy to be here. How could she be happy, when all she could think of was seeing those two cuddling up, right there in front of her in the early hours?

It was nine o'clock when she went downstairs and, going towards the long room where the formal dinner had been served, she could hear Giovanni and his mother talking. They both looked up as she entered, Giovanni immediately coming over to greet her.

'*Buon giorno, signorina,*' he murmured, looking down at her in his special way, and Emily felt like punching him.

'Oh, hello…Giovanni,' she said coolly, deliberately stepping away from him. 'Good morning, and a very happy birthday, Maria,' she added as Maria beckoned Emily to come and sit beside her at the table, which was laid for breakfast.

'Good morning, Emily,' Maria said. 'And thank you. Wasn't it a wonderful party? And I had no idea! Giovanni is too good to his mother!' She paused. 'You are looking very pretty this morning, Emily—and what an exquisite dress you were wearing last night! It looked as if it had been made just for you! You must know exactly where to shop.'

'Thank you,' Emily replied, thinking—if only you knew!

'You have very good taste,' Maria went on, 'and, by the way—did you ever manage to rescue that summer dress—the one with all the blood and dirt on it? I'm afraid I had my doubts.'

Emily smiled briefly as she took her place. 'No, I'm afraid I have to keep it for lounging around at home, or in the garden,' she said. 'You can still see the stains, though they're a bit fainter.'

'The main thing is,' Giovanni said mildly, 'that the young lady in question was not as badly hurt as it looked at the time.' He paused. 'I checked up at the hospital a couple of days later, and she's going to be fine.'

Rather shyly, Emily reached into her handbag and took out Maria's present.

'This is just a small gift, Maria,' she said. 'I'm afraid it's not likely to compete with all the amazing presents you were opening last night, but…I do wish you many happy returns of the day.' She placed it beside Maria, who immediately started untying the dainty ribbon. She looked at Emily shrewdly.

'You should never apologize when presenting someone with a gift,' Maria said. 'There was no need for you to bring me anything, but thank you…I know I shall like it very much.'

Slowly, she undid the flimsy wrapping paper and too

out the picture…and the expression on her face needed no explanation, her small gasp of pleasure as she studied the painting telling its own story. 'This is…so…beautiful…' she said quietly, obviously touched, and Giovanni broke in.

'Is that one of yours, Emily?' he asked eagerly, bending over to gaze at it.

'Yes—it was a little scene which Coral and I came across when we were out walking one day—this lovely mother goose taking all her babies down to the water for a swim.' She smiled. 'A painting is never as good as the real thing, of course, but I thought this was getting close.'

'It's really good—isn't it, Mamma? I told you about Emily's paintings… It is professional—don't you agree?'

For a few moments Maria said nothing, but continued studying the picture. When she looked up at Emily, her eyes were moist.

'This…gift…outshines anything else I may have received,' she said, 'because it is not only a delight to look at, but also it must have taken many hours to achieve this standard.' She shook her head briefly. 'Thank you very much, *carissima*. It shall be a most treasured possession.'

Somehow, the last few minutes had helped Emily restore something of her good spirits—not just because it was obvious that Maria was genuinely thrilled with the painting, but it reminded the girl that there was so much more to life than finding a partner, finding love, daring to trust. Happiness existed in so many other ways, too. When she got home, she would make much more time for her painting, she decided.

They finished their breakfast, with Emily purposely not looking at Giovanni or catching his eye, but merely contributing to the desultory conversation, and Giovanni was only too aware of her coolness. Still, it didn't bother him too much. He knew what women could be like at times… Wasn't that part of their allure?

Presently, Maria stood up and touched Emily's arm. 'Let me show you around the place,' she said pleasantly. 'I know there has not been time for you to investigate… and a walk in the cloisters will do *me* good, anyway—I'm afraid I drank a little too much wine last night!'

Giovanni stood as well. 'That's a good idea, Mamma,' he said easily, willing Emily to look at him—which she didn't, 'and I can sort out that paperwork you showed me yesterday. It shouldn't take me too long,' he added, 'but Emily and I will need an early lunch—I want to leave here about three o'clock, if that's OK.'

Maria nodded. 'Margherita knows about lunch,' she said briefly.

Presently, Maria led Emily through the courtyard towards the entrance to the cloisters. It was a lovely morning, though the season was no longer very warm, and Maria glanced approvingly at Emily's wrap, which she'd tied loosely around her shoulders. Maria smiled, touching it with her fingers.

'I said you had very good taste,' she said. 'Do you like this? It is one of ours, of course.'

Emily smiled back. 'It is my favourite wrap,' she said simply. 'All my friends are envious of it, and I…just love it. My father gave it to me,' she added.

'We have sold many like it,' Maria said. 'It is always good when a garment meets such general approval,' she added. 'And you wear it so well, Emily…casually, lovingly, just as it should be worn.'

They reached the cloisters, and now quite a cold draught greeted them as they began their stroll. Maria tucked her arm into Emily's.

'Do you have plans for your future, Emily?' she asked bluntly, and Emily was almost caught off guard, remembering Maria's rather straight way of talking.

'Oh, well…yes…sort of,' she replied guardedly. 'I hope to do more travelling—for the firm—because it is helping to boost my confidence. And…I'd like to have more time for my painting, of course—but that's a pipe dream, I'm afraid. And I enjoy making things. I make curtains for my father when he needs them—though I shan't be doing that again,' she added.

'Oh? Why is that?'

'Well, very surprisingly, he recently informed my brother and me that he is to marry again soon, so his new wife will be doing his sewing.' She paused. 'We never imagined that such a thing might happen—he and my mother were always so close and, after she died four years ago, my father vowed that no woman would ever take her place. That he would never marry again. But…life can be unpredictable. And people can change. See life differently.' She bit her lip thoughtfully. Her father, whose opinion on things, on life in general, Emily had always respected, had decided to take a gamble with his life…perhaps trusting, just a little, to fate. To venture where his heart was leading him.

'Do you mind—that he is to marry again?' Maria asked.

'Oh, no, of course not!' Emily replied at once. 'It was wonderful to see him so…relaxed. And Alice seems a very nice woman indeed. I'm sure they can be happy together. And that'll make me happy.'

'So—what about you, yourself, I mean?' Maria persisted. 'Will you marry, too, one day?'

'Sometimes I think I will, and at other times I think the opposite,' Emily replied, surprised at how comfortable she felt talking to Maria. And that made her bold enough to ask a question of her own. 'What about Giovanni?' she said lightly. 'He, too, is still single.' She looked away for a second, then, 'Who is the girl in that photograph—the one in his flat, Maria? She is very beautiful…and obviously someone very special to Giovanni.'

Maria pursed her lips for a second. 'Ah, yes—that is a picture of Paulina,' she said quietly. 'My son's wife…'

If she'd been struck by lightning, Emily couldn't have felt more shocked. The woman was his *wife?* A wife who he still loved, obviously… Their behaviour in the semi-darkness last night had said it all. 'Oh…' she said faintly. 'I had no idea that Giovanni was married.' Was she going mad…what was going on? Had she dreamed all those things he'd said to her the other night?

'Well, sadly he is not any more.' Maria's expression was grim. 'Paulina died last year—after a very short illness.' She shrugged. 'But I'm glad to say that Giovanni himself is so much better now. He was instructed by his doctors to have some time off to recover from his ordeal…and I insisted that he should have a complete rest from all his responsibilities here in Italy.' She shook her head. 'But these sad things take their own time,' she added. 'And I have hated to see him so unhappy…so down. Not like him at all, to be that way.'

Emily was totally mystified—and baffled—at why Giovanni had never thought to mention such a dramatic event in his life, or that he'd been married. How could anyone be so secretive? And if the woman in the garden hadn't been his wife—which, clearly, she couldn't have been—who was she? Obviously another enchanting female who took his fancy! But, now that Emily had started, she couldn't stop. She cleared her throat. 'Giovanni's loss must have been terrible,' she said, thinking how strange her own voice sounded. 'I'm sure they were very much in love…'

Maria's lips tightened again, in the way that Emily was beginning to recognize. 'We had known Paulina—and her family—for many years,' she said, 'and I thought she was perfect for Giovanni… In fact, I told him so on many occasions and perhaps I should not have done.' She paused before going on. 'They had been married for only two years before Paulina was taken ill…but I'm afraid things had not been going well with them for some time before that.' She clicked her tongue. 'Life is a melting pot of good things and bad things, Emily…but that is what it is. Life. And one must always hope.' She tucked her arm more firmly into Emily's, not surprised that Giovanni wanted her so badly. The girl was different from any of the others her son had known… For one thing, she was obviously a 'family' person, clearly caring and loyal, but there was also an indefinable quality about her that was very seductive—to both sexes. Maria had sensed it at once. Not to mention the fact that Emily was beautiful… But, of course, Giovanni *deserved* a beautiful woman! Of that his mother was in no doubt! It was his right! But the thing troubling Maria so deeply was that Giovanni had said he'd known from the very first that Emily was the one woman he was sure could give him back some happiness, and that if he couldn't have her, then he'd settle for no one else. That never again would he look for another woman, trust another woman to share his life. What a state of affairs! No second marriage, no second chance, no babies! Aldo was no longer in the equation, and there were no other men in the family to see that the firm continued to develop and prosper as it had done for generations! Her son's flatly stated announcement during their long chats this weekend had been Maria's worst possible birthday present! And it left her in no doubt that he meant it. Once he made up his mind—about anything—nothing would change it. But it seemed that the one thing he had to do was to change *Emily's* mind—for hadn't he said that she did not return his feelings? How could she not? How could she not see what a wonderful man Giovanni was…? Surely everything any woman could desire!

Later, as Emily, Giovanni and Maria sat outside in a sheltered corner of the patio enjoying their mid-morning coffee, Giovanni glanced across at Emily. She looked pale this morning, he thought, almost waif-like ..though he loved the red dress she was wearing. It hugged her slender neck and arms and emphasized her neat waistline. But appearances were not everything, he acknowledged, and it was impossible not to be aware of her mood. She seemed more distant than ever this morning, and it had to be all about the wretched dynasty, of course—and not being told about it before. He cursed inwardly. Why hadn't he plucked up the courage to tell her about his background earlier? Whatever had made him think that bringing her here and then telling her was a good idea? Well, her feisty reaction to the news had put him right on that point! She felt she'd been put at a disadvantage—and she hadn't liked it.

Giovanni sighed briefly as he finished his coffee. He'd always prided himself that he understood women, but he was beginning to feel that he didn't know them as well as he thought he did. And he also knew that, somehow, he was going to have to bring her round, make her forgive him for keeping her in the dark.

Giovanni had been looking forward to bringing Emily here to his home—the home he'd hoped would be hers one day—but, as he saw her staring implacably in front of her with that non-committal expression he'd often seen before,

his doubts were growing by the minute. Yet, in spite of everything, he knew that she liked him—a lot—and also
that—did he dare to even think it—she fancied him. His
whole body tensed as he recalled the erotic feel of her body
almost wrapped in his when they had been on the river, the
soft roundness of her breast in his hand, her undoubted
willingness to have travelled further. It all gave him a
blood-rush as he lived it again.

But that was then, this was now. If he was going to win
this woman over, he'd have to think of something—fast.

It was in a rather subdued mood that they made the journey
back to the UK, with Emily staring rather listlessly out of
the aircraft window while Giovanni tried, unsuccessfully,
to concentrate on the first page of his newspaper.

He cleared his throat. 'I'm really sorry that I didn't tell
you, you know, about all the stuff regarding my family,'
he began, and Emily interrupted quickly.

'There's no need to apologize,' she said flatly. 'It doesn't
matter—not one bit. I was very happy to meet Maria again,'
she added, 'and it was a pleasant and very…informative…
time for me.' Emily looked across at Giovanni, holding his
gaze, but now her tone was soft. 'I was sorry to hear of your
wife's untimely death, Giovanni,' she said, thinking that he
must still find it hard to talk about—to anyone.

Emily turned back to look out of the window again, and
Giovanni felt his blood rising in anger. Why had his
mother complicated things by talking about that to Emily?
he thought. She should have left it to him, to deal with in
his own way at the right time. He touched her arm. 'The
past is the past,' he said, 'and nothing can change that
now. It's over. Gone. The only important thing remaining
is the future, and what we make of it.'

'But the past *is* important,' Emily began, and he interrupted her.

'Only if we learn from it,' he said soberly. 'And try not to make the same mistakes again.'

It was quite late as they hailed a cab outside the airport, and Giovanni looked down at Emily. 'Thank you again, for coming with me this weekend, Emily,' he said quietly. 'I know my mother appreciated everything…and especially the painting you gave her. She hasn't stopped going on about it.'

Emily smiled briefly. 'I'm glad she liked it.'

They got into the taxi and gave the driver instructions. Then, 'I must see you tomorrow, Emily—I want to talk to you,' he added, almost desperately. He was not going to let Emily slip through his fingers, and he knew, he just *knew,* he could win her…that she would understand everything…understand him, eventually.

Emily looked up at him. 'Sorry, Giovanni, I can't possibly see you tomorrow,' she said. 'The firm are sending me to Estonia in the morning—didn't I say? I shall be away until next week.' Her voice faltered at this deliberate lie, but she was not going to see Giovanni again—this weekend had been just too much to take in. And her excuse was as good as any. She had to have some space to get her thoughts in order. She wasn't going to risk her life in this man's hands, and the first step in the procedure was to distance herself from him, forget how much she'd started to love being with him, being close to him, breathing in that subtle, evasive masculine scent that sent all her nerves twitching. Giovanni Boselli was dangerous. She wanted out!

## CHAPTER THIRTEEN

IT WAS four whole days since they'd returned to the UK and Giovanni's current commitment at the branch office was complete—there was simply no excuse for him to remain in London and he was needed in Rome, now and for the foreseeable future. So it was time to go home. But not before he'd had a chance to see Emily again and try to restore something of the position he'd thought they'd been in before. He knew she was upset with him— perhaps understandably, he accepted—but he'd never dreamed that his background, his rather exceptional status, would be such a big deal for her...that he was who he was.

Now, he looked at his watch. It was nearly lunchtime— time to decide on some action! Because they'd not exchanged a word since Monday night and he knew he couldn't bear this silence a day longer. Emily's mobile obviously had a fault, he reasoned, or else she was not answering—which he thought was unlikely, because wouldn't her firm need to contact her while she was away? He bit his lip. He didn't really want to embarrass her by ringing her office, but there was nothing else for it. He'd think of some plausible excuse...

He dialled the number, and almost at once a voice answered.

'Justin Taylor. Can I help?'

Giovanni cleared his throat. 'Oh, hi. Sorry to trouble you…Justin… It's Giovanni Boselli here. I think we met some time ago. I was wondering if you could tell me how I can get in touch with Emily. Her mobile seems constantly on the blink.' He paused. 'Could you give me the name of the hotel she's staying at? I believe she's in Tallinn at the moment.'

'No, she isn't,' Justin replied at once. 'She's not due in Estonia for another ten days.'

This unexpected piece of news nearly floored Giovanni.

'She…she isn't?' he said incredulously. 'But she told me she was going—on Tuesday—for a week.' Giovanni quickly recovered his composure. 'Oh, well, anyway…is she there?' he asked. 'Can I have a word?'

'No, you can't, I'm afraid. She's not in the office, hasn't been all week,' Justin said. 'She phoned in sick on Tuesday morning.'

Giovanni put down the phone and stared into space for a few moments, his throat constricting at the thought that Emily might be really ill. Then he shook his head briefly. But…she'd *lied* to him, about going to Estonia! But why? It was a horrible thought. She didn't need to do that. But clearly she didn't want to see him, or even speak to him, which was why she wasn't answering his calls.

He went over to the drinks cooler and poured himself a generous cup of water. He was utterly confused emotionally, and hurt beyond belief that he'd been lied to, humiliated that he'd been taken in, had believed her. But, much much worse, Giovanni couldn't bear to think that she may be really ill. He finished the drink and poured hims some more. At least she had Coral there to look after her for part of each day…unless Coral, too, had succumbed! Giovanni cursed to think that he didn't have Coral's number, to check.

Presently, his normal clear-headed thinking took over. When he left work he'd go straight over to their flat, he decided. Whatever explanation Emily had for her deviousness, he thought, he must hear it from her. He couldn't stand unresolved, unsettled matters. In his book, it was always best to get things sorted—then move on. Even if the outcome was not always the happy one you'd hoped for.

He left the office and took a cab straight to the familiar address. He glanced up at the first floor—he knew which was Emily's bedroom—and, through a tiny chink in the closed curtains, he could see a dim light. He paused outside the front door for a few moments before trying, yet again, to get Emily to answer her mobile, but with the same result.

It was almost dark by now, and Giovanni was conscious of one or two strange looks from passers-by as he stood hesitantly on the front doorstep. Looking up and down the street, he was praying that he'd suddenly see Coral coming home, but there was no sign of her and, eventually, reluctantly, he pressed lightly on the doorbell. Emily would not want to be disturbed, he appreciated that, but how else could he be sure that she was OK, or whether she needed anything? And if she was annoyed at the intrusion on her privacy, he couldn't help it. He *had* to know.

There was no response to his ring… If only she'd open her window and just talk to him, he thought desperately, just for a moment, tell him she was all right. That would be enough. But, apart from that small bedroom light, the place might have been deserted.

Standing there, Giovanni really didn't know what to do next… If theirs had been a ground-floor flat, he thought, he might even have tried breaking in! And then, quietly emerging out of the gathering gloom, someone came up the path towards him.

'Can I help you—are you looking for someone?' the man said, in a none-too-friendly voice.

Giovanni spoke quickly. 'Oh…yes.' He stood well back so as not to appear intimidating to the rather slight middle-aged man. 'My name is Giovanni Boselli, and I'm a friend of Emily's…Emily Sinclair?'

The man smiled now, inserting his key into the door. 'Ah, yes, Emily. I think they're both away,' he said. 'I haven't seen either of the girls for a few days, but then, I'm often not here myself.' He turned to look at Giovanni, who had come up behind him. 'I'm Andy Baker—I own this property.'

'Of course—I remember you called once, while I was having dinner with Emily,' Giovanni said, almost wanting to throw his arms around the man's neck in relief. He paused. 'The thing is…I believe Emily is ill in bed…I haven't been able to contact her all week, and I'm worried about her.' He hesitated. 'Do you have a spare key so that I can let myself in to check everything's OK?'

Andy couldn't help feeling sorry for him, but felt bound to express some doubt about doing what Giovanni had asked. 'Well, I don't know really…I'm only legally allowed to gain access in an emergency…' he began, and Giovanni interrupted.

'But I have a real feeling that this *is* an emergency,' he said. 'Look, if we could just open her door and call out— ask her if she's OK—there can't be any harm in that, surely?'

'Well, I suppose not,' Andy said rather reluctantly, a together the two of them went up the stairs. When they to Emily's door, they paused for a second and Giovanni tapped lightly.

'Emily…it's Giovanni. Is everything all right?' he called.

There was no reply but, as Giovanni looked down at Andy, they both heard a low moan, followed by a crash and the unmistakable tinkle of breaking glass.

'Look, we must go in,' Giovanni said, trying not to sound as desperate as he felt. 'Please—open her door.'

As if making a world-shattering decision, Andy stepped forward and selected a key from the bunch in his hand, opening the door.

They went inside and, with Andy hovering anxiously behind him, Giovanni went straight into Emily's bedroom.

She was lying on her side on the bed, the covers thrown off and with one arm dangling towards the floor, and she half-opened her eyes as she became aware that she was not alone. Then she tried to struggle up into a sitting position and Giovanni moved forward to support her, stepping over the glass from the broken tumbler on the floor. Her appearance sent shock waves through him. She was deathly pale, with her hair tousled around her face, and her eyes looked huge and almost opaque as she stared up at him.

'*Emilee-a….*' he breathed, gathering her up into his arms, and she automatically leaned into him, flopping her head against his shoulder.

'What time is it?' she whispered through dry lips. 'I must get up…'

Andy cleared his throat as he stood awkwardly by the door. 'Well…I'll be going on upstairs,' he said, turning to leave. 'Let me know if there's anything I can do… You now where I am…' he added. He paused. 'Just as well e came in, wasn't it? Poor Emily. Doesn't look too good, s she…?'

When he'd gone, Giovanni laid Emily back down and drew the covers over her gently. She looked up at him, and now she was beginning to focus more clearly.

'What are you doing here?' she croaked, her voice hoarse. Then, 'I can't remember coming to bed… What's going on?'

Giovanni sat beside her, taking her hand in his. 'How long have you been lying here by yourself?' he asked. 'Do you know what day it is?'

'It's Tuesday—isn't it?' Emily replied. 'Yes, it's Tuesday…'

'No, it's Friday, Emily. And you've obviously gone down with something.' He paused. 'Where's Coral— shouldn't she be home soon?'

Emily was wide awake and aware now, and she struggled to sit up again. 'Coral's away on a course,' she said weakly.

'So you've been here all alone for four days,' Giovanni said. 'I was getting frantic with worry because I hadn't heard from you, Emily, so I rang the office…' He didn't go on because now was not the time for explanations. What *was* needed was to make Emily more comfortable. Seeing her so helpless and vulnerable made him want to hold her close. He suddenly had no feelings of resentment about her lying to him, he realized. What did that matter now? All he felt was intense compassion and an overwhelming longing to bring her back to normal, to make her feel good again.

For the next ten minutes, Giovanni busied himself with practical matters. He cleared the small bedside table of several empty tumblers and crumpled tissues, and screwed the top back onto the half-empty bottle of tablets Emil' had obviously been taking. Then he went into the kitch and found a dustpan and brush to clear up the brol glass, before putting the kettle on to make Emily a hot drink.

When he came back, she was sitting weakly on the edge of the bed, struggling into her dressing gown, and Giovanni went across to help her.

'Oh, dear,' she said faintly. 'I'm beginning to remember everything now.' She paused. 'I woke early on Tuesday morning—and knew straight away that I couldn't go to work… I felt terrible. But I thought if I had a day in bed, I'd soon recover.' She swallowed. 'And that's really the last thing I remember. Except…I do remember going into the bathroom and getting myself water to drink…and I think I took some tablets…but that's all, really.' She looked away, not wanting to gaze into the dark eyes that she knew were staring down at her.

Giovanni put his hand on her forehead gently. 'Well, you're cool enough now, so obviously your temperature's back to normal,' he said. 'But you must be ready for something to eat. What do you fancy? What can I get you?'

By now, Emily was right back on track and she knew she had to explain about not being in Estonia. But…she'd put it off for as long as possible, she thought, so she replied quickly, 'I feel like a slice of toast with some marmalade on it. The jar is in the cupboard above the sink.' She sighed weakly. 'And I think there's bread in the fridge.'

Giovanni grinned down at her, relieved to see that Emily was obviously coming back to the real world. 'Toast and marmalade coming up,' he said, going into the kitchen.

Getting up, and feeling as if she were floating a foot off the floor, Emily tottered into the bathroom and stared at herself in the mirror. Whatever did she look like? But by now she was past caring. She filled the basin with warm water and began to wash her hands and face, drawing the sponge up around her neck and arms before smoothing some of her moisturizer onto her skin. Then she reached for her toothbrush, squeezing some paste onto it, the strong peppermint making her tongue tingle pleasantly. That made her feel a lot better. Then she took her brush and eased some of the tangles from her hair, making a face at herself in the mirror… She still looked a mess, she thought, but it would have to do for now.

It was so good to have Giovanni here, Emily thought suddenly, pausing for a second. In spite of the doubts she had about him, he could be so utterly kind and thoughtful…everything any woman could want in a man, especially in her hour of need. And at every other time too! But—and it was a big but—could they last a lifetime together, as he apparently thought they could…and would *she* ever be enough for Giovanni Boselli? There was so much he hadn't told her. So much she needed to know.

Presently, she went to sit down on the sofa, just as he came in with the toast and two mugs of tea on a tray and, as Emily started to nibble at the first food she'd had for some time, he sat on a chair opposite and watched her. Some colour had come back into her cheeks, he noticed, and her beautiful eyes, as she glanced across at him, looked clearer now and as discerning as ever.

Then she said, 'I expect you were surprised to find that I wasn't in Estonia this week.'

Giovanni shrugged, as if he'd hardly thought about it. 'Obviously some last-minute change of plan?' he suggested, trying to make it easy for her.

She stared at him for a long moment before answering him truthfully. 'No, it wasn't that,' she said slowly. 'I wanted you to think I'd be away because…because—' she swallowed '—I didn't want to see you, Giovanni.' S' sipped from her mug. 'I thought it best if...you see...I'm afraid, Giovanni,' she whispered.

'Afraid—of *me*, Emilee-a?' he said quietly.

'A bit,' she admitted, not looking at him.

Giovanni's face was expressionless. Then, 'You won't mind if I ask for an explanation?' he asked mildly. 'Are you still mad at me for not admitting sooner who my family was—is? And what my future is likely to entail?' He paused. 'Or, indeed, that I'd been married once?' he added as an afterthought.

Emily nodded slowly. 'I do still find it hard to think how anyone could avoid mentioning all that before,' she conceded, 'but it's not just that, Giovanni.'

Now he was really puzzled. 'So—what is it?' he asked.

There was a long pause before Emily spoke again. Then, 'I don't want to love you...I don't want to fall in love with someone who I'm afraid would find it hard to be faithful,' she said earnestly. 'Loyalty is the essential element which is needed to bind a relationship, to make it last for a lifetime.'

'I agree with that,' Giovanni responded at once. 'So—what are you trying to say?'

'Must I spell it out?' Emily said.

'I'm afraid you'll have to,' he said quietly.

'Well—what about that girl at the party...the one I saw you with from my window, much later on that night?' Emily said, suddenly feeling energized. 'I saw you two together, how you were holding her, kissing her...she must be someone very special to you, Giovanni.'

The slight frown which had started to form on Giovanni's features cleared briefly and he leaned forward and let out a deep sigh. 'Oh—what must you have thought, Emilee-a?' he said slowly. He shook his head. 'That very

special woman is my sister, Francesca,' he said. He took
a deep breath, realizing that there was even more for Emily
to find out about his family. 'We see Francesca very infre-
quently, thanks to her working life,' he said. 'She did a
politics degree at university and now has a high-octane job
with the government…all top secret stuff which we never
ask her about—and she wouldn't tell us, in any case. But
of course she is constantly flying all over the world, and
actually only got back from the States very late on Sunday
night—you had already gone to bed—just in time to wish
my mother a happy birthday. But she was collected again
almost before dawn to accompany the Prime Minister's en-
tourage to Japan.' Giovanni looked deadly serious for a
moment. 'Did you really think that she and I…?'

'Well, you did look very close…' Emily began hesitantly, wondering how many more surprising revelations
she was to learn. 'You seemed so deep in conversation.'

'That is certainly true,' he agreed, 'because I was telling
her all about you, Emily…about this wonderful English
girl that I'm in love with. But I also had to tell her that I
didn't think you cared too much for me…not in the way
I am yearning for.' He paused, finding it hard to go on for
a second. 'My sister has always given me good advice,'
he said, 'and her words were—*Never give up on your
heart's desire. If something feels right, go for it. Never give
up.*'

He looked so appealing, so earnest, that Emily wanted
him to hold her close…wanted to feel his arms around her
and not let her go. 'So…Francesca…has no part in the
family business?' she asked, trying to keep her voice
steady.

'No, she has never had any interest at all in fashion
how the business works,' he said. 'And my parent

spected that, respected her wishes to go it alone.' He smiled briefly. 'My mother is intensely proud of what Francesca has achieved in her own profession. After all, it isn't everyone who can say that they occasionally take tea with the Prime Minister, or who has met the President of the United States.'

There was a long silence while Emily ate the last of her toast slowly, admitting that her head was feeling almost as light as it had when she'd been suffering that temperature. But she was on an unstoppable train now, she thought. There was more she must know.

'And Paulina?' she asked steadily. 'Your wife? Tell me about her, Giovanni. I want to know everything—everything about *you*.'

His expression clouded, but only for a moment. 'That is one subject that I do not like to think about…do not like to talk about,' he said seriously, 'but I understand why I must tell you, Emilee-a. It is only right that I should.'

He had hardly touched his tea, and now he put down his mug, standing up and going across to the window, drawing aside the curtain and staring out into the night sky.

'Paulina—and Francesca—and I had been friends for many years, when we were all very young,' he said slowly. 'She was very beautiful… In fact, she looked so like Francesca they were sometimes taken for sisters.'

'Yes, I know. I've seen that photograph in your flat, Giovanni,' Emily said.

'I'd never really imagined that our relationship would develop into something deeper,' he went on, 'but some-´mes life takes on a rhythm which is difficult to stop. She ıs…very much in love with me, that was the trouble… ` was like a loyal dog, looking at me with those big …and I found it hard to tell her that I did not feel quite the same way about her. I did try,' he said, 'and she even threatened to kill herself on one occasion.' He paused. 'Everyone else in the family—' Giovanni did not mention his mother '—told me so many times that we would be the perfect match, and I tried to believe that because I hated having to reject Paulina. To be rejected is the most hurtful thing.' Emily glanced up briefly. Yes, she thought, she would wholeheartedly agree with that.

'So—we got married,' Giovanni said, 'and life was pretty good…it was OK. But Paulina changed…she developed into a woman who was never satisfied with what she had, what she was given. She was constantly shopping, buying clothes, shoes, handbags, things she didn't really need or want…the perfect example of someone who was trying to fill her life with something she was lacking.' Giovanni paused for so long that Emily looked up curiously. This was hurting him, she thought, hurting him to speak about. But presently he continued, and his voice was sombre.

'I realized, too late, that it was all my fault,' he said. 'Because I neglected her—shamefully. I was working all hours—the business was going through a difficult patch—something that only I could really deal with. There was no one else, and my mother is no longer young. I could not expect too much of her.' He sighed, then, 'I always gave Paulina whatever she wanted—paid all her bills without question, but it started to become serious and I had no idea how to handle it. Money is not everything, and it can become a monster—and that is what it became for us. The more Paulina had, the more she wanted. I tried to talk to her about it, but then she accused me of being mean.' He gave a short, harsh laugh. 'The only thing I was me about was not giving my wife the attention she deserve giving her time so that we could be together properly, to enjoy our lives as other married couples do.' He shook his head. 'At the time, I was totally stressed, my nerves hanging by a thread, or so it seemed. Then the unimaginable thing happened—Paulina developed a serious medical problem which no one suspected, and she died within a few months. Died before I could put things right between us, before I could make up for my lack of—thoughtfulness—of attentiveness—which is every woman's right, surely? I had put the family business—our wonderful, sometimes cursed dynasty—before more important issues like the feelings, the comfort of my wife. And I am left with a deep sense of shame. I can never forgive myself,' he replied.

There was such a long pause after that that Emily looked up at him, frowning.

'But the very worst thing, Emily, was something I have never told anyone before—anyone at all,' he emphasized. He swallowed. 'During one of her many outbursts, which were becoming more and more frequent, Paulina told me that she'd never been in love with me at all, anyway. What she was in love with was what I owned—and what she wanted access to. She said that from a young age she'd been determined that one day I would marry her.' He turned slowly and looked down at Emily. 'But, in spite of all that, I am left with a deep sense of shame…a sense of failure. And I can never forgive myself,' he repeated.

He came back to sit down beside Emily, whose throat had formed such a hard lump of sympathy she couldn't speak. But she took his hand gently as he went on.

'So—I was forced to take a long leave of absence from work recently and, apart from a couple of visits I made to the UK office, I've spent much of the time in Rome with friends, doing simple things like minding shops belonging to other people and generally chilling out. Which is when I met you, Emilee-a, *carissimo*.' He squeezed her hand tightly. 'And, even at that early point, I felt a surge of something…a quite irrational hope that some miracle might happen for me.' He hesitated. 'But perhaps, now, you can understand my reluctance to say too much about the past,' he said slowly, 'though it was never meant to be a secret…something to be held back. But I like to think that I've learned from it. I will never make the same mistake again. Any woman who entrusts her life with me will never be short-changed,' he added, thinking that he was only going to give himself one more chance to prove that—and it had everything to do with Emily.

She turned her head and looked right up into his eyes.

'I hope you *will* forgive yourself, one day, Giovanni,' she said. 'Carrying guilt around with you for too long isn't healthy. It doesn't achieve anything in the long run.'

'I know you are right,' he said, 'but I need someone to help me with that, Emily…it isn't something I can do by myself.' He looked down at her, his whole body tensing with desire at her closeness, at the soft feel of her body, at the sweet, warm smell of her skin. And, sensing that she wouldn't stop him, he tucked her in tighter, reaching for her lips and kissing her gently, cautiously.

And Emily felt her heart breaking into tiny little pieces inside her…little pieces of unbelievable, undeniable surrender. Resting against him pensively, she wondered whether she dared to ask one final question…

She turned her face to look up at him. 'Whose negligee was that, hanging in the bathroom of your flat, Giovanni' she asked, trying not to make the question sound in a way accusing, and he smiled down at her.

'That's my sister's,' he said. 'Francesca leaves it there permanently for when she uses the flat as a flying stop-over.' He answered the question as casually as Emily had asked it, and for a few moments there was a comfortable silence as they both relaxed there in the gentle comfort of the modest room.

Suddenly, neither of them could bear it any longer, and now his lips came down on to Emily's and he kissed her, properly, urgently, with such heightened ardour that it left her senses reeling. And Emily responded without hesitation… No man had ever filled her with such a passionate longing, such yearning…such unbelievable excitement.

In a moment, he whispered, 'Tell me you love me, Emilee-a, tell me I'm not hoping for something which will never be mine. Tell me that you will be my wife, my life…my everything—for ever…'

And, at last, in a breathless, timeless moment, Emily murmured, 'I have been trying *not* to love you, Giovanni, but I can't keep it up any longer.' She paused. 'Of course I love you,' she said, adding softly, 'How could I help it?' and his dark eyes, those mesmerizing windows of his soul, glistened with unshed tears of pleasure and happiness at the words he'd been longing, hoping, praying to hear.

But would his family ever accept her? Emily thought, as Giovanni's lips claimed hers again. She instinctively felt that Maria was a formidable woman… She could be a formidable enemy… What if she, Emily, wasn't deemed good enough for the illustrious Bosellis? She drew away and looked up at him. 'Do you…do you think I would fit in, Giovanni?' she asked. 'Come up to standard, shall we say…?'

'What on earth do you mean, Emily?' he asked.

'I'm talking about Maria…your mother. I know she

has strong views on important matters. Would I ever be good enough for her remarkable son?'

Giovanni gave a short laugh. 'My mother is as much in love with you as I am, Emily! Truly, I mean it. I have had long chats with her, and she has told me that if I can persuade you to be my wife, it will be her happiest day!' He paused. 'She liked being with you, talking to you. And she could not believe that the picture you gave her was not a copy…but that you had painted it yourself, using your own memory and imagination. And my mother is a very perceptive woman,' he went on, 'she knows a gifted artist when she meets one.' Giovanni's face broke into a broad grin. 'I think she would love to have you on board, on our design team…you'd be someone with fresh, modern ideas, and every company needs new blood from time to time.' He paused. 'Just think,' he said, 'it would be like turning full circle—you and me, the two of us, Emilee-a, taking on what my great-grandparents began all those years ago! Isn't that an amazing thought? Besides,' he added mischievously, 'Antonio needs some heirs—and I think you and I, together, can sort that one out. Only if that's what you want, too, of course,' he said quickly. 'Your feelings will always come first.' Giovanni's eyes glistened and, looking up at him, Emily thought, not for the first time, that she would never again know such an achingly desirable man. And someone who, at last, she *was* going to trust. Because she knew that she could. She remembered the words her father had used that day…that, if he'd waited much longer, he may have lost Alice for ever… Well, Emily wasn't going to hesitate any longer.

What was she waiting for? She knelt up on the sofa and put her arms around his neck, almost collapsing into him as she offered him her parted lips to be kissed again.

be tasted…and immediately his hands reached under her flimsy nightwear and roamed over her body, making every one of her nerves tingle as he caressed her back and her bare shoulders, sliding his fingers over the creamy softness of her breasts…gently at first, then with increasing passion, until Emily was forced to draw back reluctantly. Now was not the time, she thought breathlessly, even though their desire for each other was painful. Their love-making—which she knew would be beautiful and amazing beyond her wildest dreams—must wait for just a little while longer.

'Will…will this time next year do—for the first baby?' she asked teasingly. 'Is the firm prepared to wait that long—if we're lucky enough to produce any, that is?' she added.

Giovanni reached for her again. 'Don't worry about that,' he said darkly. 'Don't you know what my friends call me? I'm known throughout the entire world as "Lucky Gio". And, at this precise moment, Emilee-a, I *know* that my luck will never get better than this!'

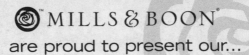

MILLS&BOON
# MODERN™

## On sale 15th January 2010

### THE WEALTHY GREEK'S CONTRACT WIFE
*by Penny Jordan*

With her last pennies in her pocket, Elizabeth arrives in
Greece to fight for what is hers. Her adversary, Ilios Manos,
will show her mercy if she will take his name!

### CASTELLANO'S MISTRESS OF REVENGE
*by Melanie Milburne*

Ava McGuire has nothing but crippling debts and a scandalous
proposition, for men like Marc Castellano don't forgive –
they get revenge…

### THE KONSTANTOS MARRIAGE DEMAND
*by Kate Walker*

Ruthless billionaire Nikos Konstantos has built himself back up
from scratch and will demand what was rightfully his…
Sadie Carteret!

### BRAZILIAN BOSS, VIRGIN HOUSEKEEPER
*by Maggie Cox*

Marianne Lockwood is mesmerised by her boss, but scarred
Eduardo de Souza is holding dark secrets and it's only a
matter of time before she finds out the truth…

### PURE PRINCESS, BARTERED BRIDE
*by Caitlin Crews*

Luc Garnier has finally got the princess he wanted – Gabrielle is
invaluable and he is increasingly determined to find the wanton
within and leave his pure princess in total disarray!

# millsandboon.co.uk Community

# *Join Us!*

The Community is the perfect place to meet and chat to kindred spirits who love books and reading as much as you do, but it's also the place to:

- ■ **Get the inside scoop from authors about their latest books**
- ■ **Learn how to write a romance book with advice from our editor**
- ■ **Help us to continue publishing the best in women's fiction**
- ■ **Share your thoughts on the books we publish**
- ■ **Befriend other users**

**Forums:** Interact with each other as well as authors, editors and a whole host of other users worldwide.

**Blogs:** Every registered community member has their own blog to tell the world what they're up to and what's on their mind.

**Book Challenge:** We're aiming to read 5,000 books and have joined forces with The Reading Agency in our inaugural Book Challenge.

**Profile Page:** Showcase yourself and keep a record of your recent community activity.

**Social Networking:** We've added buttons at the end of every post to share via digg, Facebook, Google, Yahoo, chnorati and de.licio.us.

*www.millsandboon.co.uk*

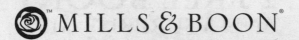

# 2 FREE BOOKS
## AND A SURPRISE GIFT

We would like to take this opportunity to thank you for reading this Mills & Boon® book by offering you the chance to take TWO more specially selected books from the Modern™ series absolutely FREE! We're also making this offer to introduce you to the benefits of the Mills & Boon® Book Club™—

- **FREE home delivery**
- **FREE gifts and competitions**
- **FREE monthly Newsletter**
- **Exclusive Mills & Boon Book Club offers**
- **Books available before they're in the shops**

Accepting these FREE books and gift places you under no obligation to buy, you may cancel at any time, even after receiving your free books. Simply complete your details below and return the entire page to the address below. You don't even need a stamp!

**YES** Please send me 2 free Modern books and a surprise gift. I understand that unless you hear from me, I will receive 4 superb new books every month for just £3.19 each, postage and packing free. I am under no obligation to purchase any books and may cancel my subscription at any time. The free books and gift will be mine to keep in any case.

Ms/Mrs/Miss/Mr_____ Initials _____

Surname _____

Address _____

_____

_____ Postcode _____

Send this whole page to: Mills & Boon Book Club, Free Book Offer FREEPOST NAT 10298, Richmond, TW9 1BR